"I must go," Helga said, and her voice broke on the words. They stared at each other, then Frank caught her to him, crushing her in his arms, bruising her with his violence.

"I love you," he said again and again, "I love you, and I haven't the courage to take you and make you belong to me. I am a coward, Helga, but, oh God, how I love you!"

He kissed her almost brutally until the blood came flooding into her cheeks and she lay breathing tumultuously in his arms. As suddenly as he had seized her, Frank let her go.

He almost threw her from him, turning away and pressing his hands to his temples.

Pyramid Books
by
BARBARA CARTLAND

THE ADVENTURER

Barbara Cartland

PYRAMID BOOKS ▲ NEW YORK

THE ADVENTURER

A PYRAMID BOOK

Copyright © 1977 by Barbara Cartland

Pyramid edition published August 1977

Printed in the United States of America

Pyramid Books are published by Pyramid Publications (Harcourt Brace Jovanovich, Inc.). Its trademarks, consisting of the word "Pyramid" and the portrayal of a pyramid, are registered in the United States Patent Office.

Pyramid Publications
(Harcourt Brace Jovanovich, Inc.)
757 Third Avenue, New York, N.Y. 10017

AUTHOR'S NOTE

I wrote this book in 1938 in a determined effort to make it different to any of the romantic novels I had written previously. Entitled *But Never Free,* it tried to portray a man's struggle to free himself from his past and find his soul.

At the time the book evoked quite a lot of comment and interest. I think it is still an absorbing story as the hero's character develops and alters.

Whatever else Frank might be, he is very human, and the temptation to make money during and after the war from the bereaved was something which actually occurred.

If you expect a usual Barbara Cartland hero, do not read *The Adventurer*—this man is different.

CHAPTER ONE

1902

The barrel-organ at the end of the street was grinding out a popular tune.

The music mingled with the noise of distant traffic and came intermittently through the half-opened window to where Frank Swinton was sitting writing.

By the empty fireplace, the hearth of which was decorated with paper creased and outspread fanwise, a young woman sat knitting.

She was quiet, save for the occasional click of her needles and the slight sound of her breathing.

There was a call outside of "Emily," and the woman rose, put down her knitting in the chair she had been sitting in, and walked out of the room shutting the door behind her.

Frank yawned, stretched his arms above his head and stared out of the window.

At twenty-two he was what was commonly called "tied to his mother's apron strings," but the strings which held him were not only those of affection but of poverty.

With a sudden gesture of disgust he pushed back his chair and getting to his feet surveyed the room around him and then himself in the oval mahogany-framed mirror over the mantelpiece.

His reflection stared at him against the background

of grey gloom. It was too dark by now to see clearly, but he knew his features only too well: the dark, rather untidy hair above the square well-shaped forehead, his mouth, too large, which nevertheless had a certain attraction when he was smiling or animated, and the firm chin.

Not really a handsome face, but supported by a tall, well-set-up body, which would have given any man presence and distinction.

"One day I will do something," Frank promised his reflection.

The door of the room opened and a shaft of light heralded the entrance of his mother carrying a lamp.

"I am sorry to keep you so long in the dark, dear," she said gently, "but the lamps wanted filling and I forgot to do it this morning."

She carried the lamp with its round opaque globe to the centre table and arranged it on a small mat of crocheted lace. When she had put it down she went to the window and pulled down the blind before drawing the heavy, velvet-tasselled curtains.

"How are you getting on with your work?" she said, seeing the scattered books and sheets of paper.

"I am not going to pass the exam," Frank said bluntly.

His mother turned anxiously at the sound of the unhappiness in his voice.

She was small and thin, with ill-kept hands worn by housework and greying hair dressed badly over a frame above her forehead.

"What is the matter, darling?" she asked.

"It's just that I'm sick and tired of working at something which I know I shall never be any use at," Frank answered. "I'm not cut out for business, for this sort of business anyway."

Mrs. Swinton sighed; she went across the room and sat down in a chair.

"But if you don't do this, Frank," she said, "what are

8

you going to do? My dear, I know it isn't the sort of work for which you are fitted. If only you could have gone to the University things might have been different."

Frank smiled bitterly; he had heard this remark often before.

"There wasn't much chance of that, was there?"

"You know there wasn't," his mother replied. "If only your father . . ."

"Where is he, by the way?" Frank asked as she paused.

"He has not got back yet," Mrs. Swinton answered, not looking at her son but at her hands as if they held a sudden interest for her.

"Well, that's nothing new," Frank said grimly.

"Don't let us discuss it," his mother said quickly. "Perhaps it will be all right tonight. Let's talk about you, darling. What would you like to do . . . if we had the money, I mean?"

"What's the point of even thinking about it?" Frank answered almost savagely. "We haven't the money and are never likely to have it."

"Oh, darling, I hate knowing that this cramped life is all I have been able to give you."

His mother's love for him made her eyes shine in the lamplight, and on an impulse Frank moved across to her and putting his arm around her shoulders gave her an affectionate squeeze.

"Don't you worry," he said. "Something will happen one day, you see if it doesn't."

The opening of the door made them both start and they faced Emily almost guiltily, for their affection was a thing best hidden from her.

Five years older than Frank, his sister Emily at twenty-seven was resigned where he was discontented, but her bitterness, made her a thorn in the flesh of her own family.

Immediately on her entrance Frank took his arm

9

from his mother's shoulders and started to tidy his books at his desk.

"Really, Mother," Emily said, "you might have waited for me to carry the lamp for you. You know what the doctor said about your heart, and the stairs from the kitchen are much too steep for you to manage the lamp."

Any consideration or kindliness in her words was belied by the fault-finding tone in which they were uttered.

"It is all right, dear," her mother replied. "I knew you were busy and I managed quite well."

"I can't see the point of having the doctor here if you can't do what he says. It's a waste of money, if you ask me," Emily said, taking up her discarded knitting.

"Well, nobody's asking you to pay him, anyway," Frank said.

"That comes well from you," Emily said sarcastically. "It's a pity you don't work a bit harder and help the family exchequer."

"Now, children, children," Mrs. Swinton said wearily, "don't start scrapping at each other. You know how I dislike it."

"The trouble with Emily," her son said, "is that she wants a home of her own but no man is such a fool as to provide one for her."

"Mother, I won't have Frank talking to me like this," Emily said furiously.

Then as Frank gave a sudden humourless laugh at her discomfiture she turned and rushed out of the room, slamming the door behind her.

There was silence when she had gone. After a moment Mrs. Swinton said:

"Frank, dear, you mustn't, you know how touchy she is. She feels that she is becoming an old maid and minds it."

"Heaven knows we all have to suffer for it! She's unbearable, Mother, she is really. It's nag, nag, nag, from morning till night. How you stand it all day I don't know."

"Poor Emily," his mother answered, "Perhaps I have made her discontented too by my ambitions."

"Nonsense!" Frank answered. "Why, you were quite well off when she was born, and happy. You were happy, that first year of marriage?"

"Yes, dear, of course I was happy," Mrs. Swinton said quickly, but Frank knew that she lied.

The clock on the mantelpiece struck ten.

"It's getting late," Mrs. Swinton said, looking up at it anxiously, as if she thought there was some likelihood of its reassuring her.

"Well, there's no point in your keeping Father's supper ready, that's one thing," Frank said.

"That's true," his mother answered, and getting to her feet went towards the door.

At half-past ten, a single stroke made them all three glance towards the clock, then turn again to their occupations.

At eleven o'clock the same thing happened, yet none of them gave the slightest indication of going to bed.

It was nearly midnight before the clatter of horse's hooves and the jingle of harness coming up the road stiffened them into startled attention.

There was the noise of a cab being drawn up outside the front door and Mrs. Swinton uttered a sound which was half-sob and half-groan before she hurried from the sitting-room into the narrow passage dimly lit by one flickering smoky lamp.

Emily followed her as far as the open door, then stood waiting apprehensively yet with a kind of curious detachment, as if she had little doubt but that her fears would be realized.

Only Frank remained seated, listening but showing neither anxiety nor distress.

As Mrs. Swinton opened the front door there was the sound of a gruff, uneducated voice, and then with the

11

ejaculations, "Take it easy, sir, it's all right," "Give us a 'and, m'm," there were sounds of someone being supported into the house.

Only when a drunken voice demanded thickly— "What the devil are you doing?"—did Frank rise slowly to his feet and say to Emily in a low voice:

"Do they want me to help?"

"Of course not," Emily answered sharply, and lowering her voice till it was little more than a whisper: "You know you only irritate him."

"Come along, Edward, we must get you up to bed," Mrs. Swinton said clearly, her voice unnaturally calm, but it was the cabman who answered her with "That's right, mum, I'll 'elp yer."

It was obviously no easy progress, for there were groans and bumps and occasional oaths before finally a crash on the ceiling overhead told Frank and Emily that the bedroom had been reached.

A few seconds later the cabman descended and waited in the hall, breathing heavily, until Mrs. Swinton came down to pay him what was due and add a small tip.

Only when the front door shut out his burly figure and the clatter of the horse's hooves was dying away in the distance, did Emily relax her vigil to burst into tears and run, sobbing audibly, upstairs to her own bedroom two floors above.

Frank went to his mother. She was standing in the hall, her worn leather purse in her hand, but she was not looking at its meagre contents but pressing her other hand against her side as if in pain.

"Are you all right, Mother?" he asked anxiously.

There were little beads of sweat on Mrs. Swinton's forehead, and it was a moment before she could answer.

Frank put his arm round her and drew her into the sitting-room.

"I must go to your father," she said, but he forced her down into the chair.

"Wait a moment until you are rested," he commanded. "I am a fool. I ought not to have let you help him up the stairs. You know what the doctor said."

"It upsets him if he sees either of you children when he is like that," Mrs. Swinton replied. "It's no use making him worse. He will sleep now."

"Oh, he'll sleep all right," Frank answered bitterly.

He knew that it was his mother who would remain awake all night beside the stupefied, almost senseless body of her husband.

"Would you like a drink of water?" he asked a moment later, as he saw the colour was returning to his mother's face and that her laboured breathing was subsiding.

"I'm all right, dear," she answered, and patted his hand. "Don't worry."

"How much did the cab cost?" Frank asked.

His mother took up the purse resting in her lap.

"Five-and-six," she answered, and there was a note of despair in her voice.

"This can't go on!" Frank said savagely, but Mrs. Swinton, getting slowly to her feet, answered:

"There is nothing one can do about it, my dear, except manage until the first of the month."

* * *

Lying awake in his small back room, Frank heard the hours strike from a distant clock. He could not sleep, and he had flung back the bedclothes, lying partially naked in the hope that what air there was would refresh him.

His thoughts would not let him rest. It was not only the events of the evening that worried him—they, after all, were a familiar occurrence.

Seldom a month passed without his father having one of these bouts of drunkenness when he would manage to spend every penny of the available household cash.

Frank had grown used to the spectacle of his father either unconscious or truculently drunk, just as he was used to the inevitable fit of repentance the following day when Edward Swinton would try to ingratiate himself with his family.

What really worried Frank was the thought of his mother. It was only in the last three months that he and Emily had become aware that she was keeping secret from them the really dangerous state of her health.

She suffered from heart trouble, aggravated by bad feeding, anæmia, and hard work, and when pressed for the truth the doctor had admitted quite frankly that it was only a question of time before she collapsed altogether.

All the years of her married life Mrs. Swinton had worked like a servant, unpaid and without a servant's privileges.

An orphan, she had been brought up by an uncle and aunt long since dead, and had considered herself fortunate in attracting the attention of a handsome young officer in a famous regiment.

Little more than a year after their marriage, however, he was cashiered for striking one of his superior officers when he was drunk.

Fortunately he had a small private income on which they could retire into obscurity, but this quickly dwindled when Edward Swinton, humiliated and resentful, indulged in wild bursts of dissipation in the attempt to seek forgetfulness.

Time after time his debts contracted in such a manner had been paid out of capital until finally there was nothing left save a small pittance inherited from his mother, which was fortunately in trust.

This money was paid to him monthly and it became eventually all that stood between the Swinton family and the workhouse.

When his son was born, after the first horror at there being another mouth to feed in their strained economic

14

conditions, Edward Swinton pulled himself together and attempted for a short while to find some employment.

Soon, however, he drifted into a lethargic despondency alternating with periods when he could bear his existence no longer and he sought relief in drink.

The remonstrances, the tears, and the prayers of his wife had less and less effect on him.

It was true that when sober he was sorry for what he had done, but at the time such penitence was invariably due to an aching head and a disordered stomach.

The only sign that he had some semblance of decency left was that however bad his condition the presence of either of his children aroused him to fury.

Occasionally when he was normal he sought the companionship of his son, but he could not help being aware that any feelings Frank had for him were certainly not affectionate.

From the moment of his birth Frank had meant everything to his mother.

He had been born at a particular time of stress. She had not wanted a baby, and in fact had almost given way to despair when she had been finally certain that she was to have one.

There was no money and Edward was being more troublesome than usual, indeed just before Frank was born his drunkenness had terminated in delirium tremens and she and the doctor had spent two nights and days striving to keep him from killing himself.

Then all the frustrated love in her seemed to find an outlet in Frank.

Strangely enough, born into such a miserable household, he was a strong, happy baby, seemingly content with his existence and ready to smile and coo at all the world. It was little wonder that Mrs. Swinton loved him.

Even less surprising was it that Emily should immediately have taken what was almost a violent dislike to the child.

Frank, as a tiny child, had sensed Emily's animosity

towards him and had turned away from the few tentative attempts she had made at friendship.

The two children had been fairly well educated, at the cost of hidden and unimaginable sacrifices on the part of their mother.

There had indeed been times when the house had been almost bare of furniture until the first of the month brought the eagerly awaited cheque.

Food was always scarce, the easiest economy was through the larder, yet they could have managed had it not been for Edward's continual outbursts of extravagance.

For Mrs. Swinton they were nightmares which pursued her from one occasion to the next. For days after one of his bouts she would start at a ring of the front door-bell or the rattle of letters being put into the box.

Bills were not just to be dreaded; they were monsters that devoured the food, light and heat which by rights were hers and her children's.

"What will become of us?" Frank wondered, as he had wondered so often before.

As a small boy when he had first become aware of what sort of man his father was and of the unhappiness he gave his mother, he had prayed continuously and earnestly that his father might die.

As he had grown older it had seemed to him, in spite of his mother's teaching and of his own boyhood faith, that there could be no God who could allow such things to happen.

The houses in Edward Street, dingy and in need of repair, were nevertheless well built, and Frank, sleeping in the room which adjoined that of his father and mother, could only occasionally hear the sound of heavy snoring through the walls.

Except when his father was angry he could not distinguish their voices.

Tonight it was very quiet in the house. Above him Emily was asleep in her tiny attic bedroom next to the boxroom, where odds and ends of the household were kept in the hope that one day they might be useful or saleable.

He thought about his mother. So often he had visualized himself earning a vast income or inheriting a fortune from some source or other, and he had imagined the way he and his mother would spend it together.

There was something about Mrs. Swinton which was made for luxury; there were a softness and a femininity about her which were lacking in her daughter.

For himself Frank's thoughts soared into the wildest dreams of gaiety and extravagance.

He saw himself well dressed, a person of importance, going here and there, visiting places, travelling, meeting amusing, interesting people, outstanding amongst them and of interest to everyone with whom he came in contact.

His thoughts were suddenly interrupted by a crash. He listened. There was silence. It sounded like someone falling, he thought.

Had his father awakened and become uproarious?— it would not be the first time that things had been broken and his mother terrified.

But it seemed to him that the crash had come not from the bedroom but from some other part of the house. The bathroom was on the half-landing, perhaps the door had swung to.

He settled himself to recapture his disrupted dreams and then some uneasiness, some strange fear, made him get out of bed and light a candle. The yellow light dazzled his eyes for a moment and threw great shadows round the room.

Leaving it beside his bed Frank moved quietly towards the door.

There was still no further sound and he hesitated before turning the handle; at last he did so cautiously. He had no desire to bump into his father should he have come out of the bedroom.

17

He opened the door and looked down the stairs. Everything seemed very quiet; then in the light shining from behind him he had a vague impression of something on the stairs.

He pulled the door open wider and then rushed forward, for huddled below him with one arm outstretched was his mother.

She had evidently fallen coming from the bathroom, the candle she had been carrying had been flung from its socket, while the candle-stick was beside her.

She was obviously in a dead faint. Frank tried to rouse her, he managed to lift her into his arms so that he could carry her up the short flight into his own room.

Her head fell back against his arm as he carried her into his room and put her down on his bed.

Frank went to the washstand and poured out a glass of water but as he turned again towards the bed he was struck by the pallor of her face and the limpness of her arms; one had fallen over the side of the bed until the fingers nearly touched the floor.

On a sudden impulse before he went to her he shut his door. He would look after her himself, he would not call Emily.

He raised her head and tried to get some drops of water between her teeth, but it was impossible and he laid her down again wondering if he had better get the doctor.

Something made him feel for her heart and as he did so he knew with a complete certainty, more clearly than if he had been told, that his mother was dead . . .

* * *

It was nearly three hours later that the dawn coming through the thin, unlined curtains, dwarfed the light of the candle into insignificance.

Frank roused himself from his knees where he had

18

been half-kneeling, half-crouching, with his head on the bed. How long he had been there he did not know.

His mother's hand which he held in his was already cold and he had difficulty in crossing her hands over her breast.

Weary, with cramped limbs, he moved towards the window and drew back the curtains a little way. It was a clear, bright morning; soon the sun would be rising over the housetops into a cloudless sky.

He turned back into the room. There were no tears in his eyes but his eyelids stung and felt dry and brittle as though they had been strained.

For a short time he stood indecisive, then rapidly he dressed himself. He took down an old Gladstone bag from the top of the wardrobe where it had been for so long a time that it was covered with dust and the catch had grown rusty from disuse.

Some of his long-discarded clothes were inside it. These he threw on the floor, replacing them with clothes which were in his drawers and a winter overcoat which hung in the cupboard.

His preparations took a little less than quarter of an hour and when he had finished he turned towards the bed, dropped on his knees beside his mother and kissed her cold forehead.

"Good-bye, darling," he said aloud in a voice which sounded hoarse and strange.

Without looking back he picked up his bag and walked quietly down the stairs, opened the front door, and went out into the deserted street.

CHAPTER TWO

1911

There were great vases of flowers standing on the heavy mahogany furniture, but on the huge carved desk which occupied the centre of the room there was only a small vase filled with white rosebuds.

Every now and then Helga, looking up from her work, glanced at them and half-smiled before she bent her head again to the task of writing addresses on the great pile of envelopes waiting at her elbow.

The sunshine glinted on the wide, heavy plait which was coiled tightly round her small head. She wore a black dress with collar and cuffs of white.

In her face, pretty as it was, she showed the capability which was reflected again in her firm, clear handwriting.

She glanced up as the footman entered.

"What is it, William?" she asked.

"The messenger has arrived from Sir Alfred, miss," he answered.

"He is late," Helga said severely. "Ask him to hurry, will you? Sir Alfred is waiting for these papers."

She handed the man a large sealed envelope, and as soon as he was gone she locked up the drawer from which she had taken it, and placed the key securely on the old-fashioned gold chatelaine which she wore hanging beneath the wide black patent-leather belt encircling her small waist.

She was not, however, to remain long uninterrupted.

There was a knock at the door and when she called out "Come in," a large fat woman in a print dress and white starched apron entered.

Helga turned to face the cook who ruled the basement of Sir Alfred's house with a rod of iron.

"Is anything wrong, Mrs. Dawkins?" she questioned.

"There is, miss," the cook answered, with a tightly pursed mouth that promised trouble below stairs.

"Not the kitchen-maid again?" Helga said anxiously.

"It most certainly is," Mrs. Dawkins replied. "I won't hold with impertinence in my kitchen any more than I will hold with such goings-on by them as is under me. It was half-past ten before Ellen came in last night and when I spoke to her about it this morning she said as how it was none of my business."

She snorted before she said, "She must go, Miss. I'm sorry, after the trouble you have had to get me one. She's a good worker, I won't say as she's not, but young girls must learn their place or be without one, that's what I says."

"I can't understand it, Mrs. Dawkins," Helga said soothingly, "after all the trouble you have taken over her too, and she was beginning to turn out such a good little cook. Supposing I speak to her and she apologizes, do you think you could give her another chance?"

"I can't see that it would do any good, Miss," Mrs. Dawkins replied, "I have spoken to her before."

"Well, let me try this time," Helga pleaded. "I know I am asking you to be kind, but then you always are. The girl has come from an unhappy home and if you turn her away now goodness knows what will happen to her. I will give her a good talking to and she will apologize for everything, I promise you."

Mrs. Dawkins wavered and was lost.

"Very well, Miss," she said, "just this once, but make it quite clear that this is her last chance."

"Oh, Mrs. Dawkins, that is kind of you!" Helga said. "I think the truth of the matter is that you spoil the girls under you and they take advantage."

"I shouldn't be at all surprised," Mrs. Dawkins said grudgingly.

"Well, send Ellen to me this afternoon when you have finished with her," Helga said, "and I will give her a good scolding."

"Thank you, Miss," the cook said, moving with dignity towards the door.

Helga sighed. It was no easy task at twenty-five to run a house of sixteen servants, but she had managed it competently for nearly three years.

She knew that Sir Alfred Steene was not only satisfied with her but relied on her for the harmony besides the well-being of the household. It had seemed at first that she had undertaken an impossible task.

Three years ago, faced with the almost impossible task of finding employment, she had come over from Germany, going to Sir Alfred for help.

He had known her father both as a business acquaintance and as a friend, in the days when Baron Hildergard had been a rich and powerful figure in German industry.

The disgrace which was attached to his name after his sudden death had driven his only daughter away from the friends she knew and from the sympathy, as well as the scorn, of those with whom she had associated so happily during her girlhood.

Fortunately she spoke English and had enjoyed part of several summer Seasons in London, but even so the problem of finding employment was not easy and she was really at her wits' end to know what to do.

She had come to Park Lane one dull January morning. She had arrived in the middle of a domestic crisis, for Sir Alfred, like many another clever man, who could

22

deal with any trouble in office or business, was helpless and miserable while a household storm raged around him.

He saw Helga, after she had been kept waiting for some time; while she talked and told him of her plight her spirits fell lower with despondency for she saw that he was hardly listening to her, his mind obviously occupied with other affairs.

Suddenly he said to her:

"Who looked after your house in Germany? I remember it well. I was very comfortable when I stayed with your father."

"I have run it ever since I was eighteen," Helga answered, a little puzzled by the question, which seemed entirely irrelevant. "After my mother died my father's sister lived with us until I grew up and then she returned to Bavaria, for she missed the mountains and hated the city."

"You engaged the servants?" Sir Alfred asked.

"Of course," Helga said with a smile. "I am very domesticated. All women have to be in my country. Also I used to help my father with all his work. He always said I was just as good as any of his secretaries.

"Do you think," she said hesitatingly, with a sudden glimmer of hope, "that I could find a post of that sort in England? I didn't think of it before but perhaps—"

"Of course," Sir Alfred interrupted, "it is here. From today, my dear child, you become my housekeeper-secretary."

"Do you really mean it?" Helga exclaimed.

She jumped to her feet and she looked so pretty and so young in her large feather-trimmed velvet hat that another man might have felt some anxiety at his decision.

But Sir Alfred was used to making up his mind swiftly. He felt no misgivings.

He had amassed a large fortune by this very method and it was with the air of a man who discharges a heavy burden on to someone else's shoulders that he patted Helga's hand.

He assured her that she would give every satisfaction, and marched her triumphantly up the stairs to interview his daughter.

Edith Steene was fifteen, an ugly sallow-faced child who looked un-English and who took an instantaneous dislike to every governess whom her father engaged for her.

Lady Steene had died only six months before but she had been little more successful than her husband in choosing congenial teachers for her daughter.

Complaints of trouble, however, had not been allowed to reach Sir Alfred's ears, and he imagined pathetically that it was due to his own inefficiency after his wife's death that Edith was so troublesome.

By one of those curious tricks of fate which cannot be explained, Edith took a liking to Helga which in the years to come was to develop into almost adoration.

Perhaps Helga's looks had something to do with the matter. Edith was plain, she was too thin, and although she was short she gave the appearance of having outgrown her strength.

All her life she had been surrounded by elderly, painstaking women who, doubtless possessing hearts of gold, were nevertheless outwardly unprepossessing.

Helga, with her golden hair, her pink and white complexion, and her lovely dark-blue eyes, was to Edith the personification of all the fairy stories she had ever read.

To her, indeed, Helga was the first thing of beauty she had seen in her luxurious and overwhelming home.

Lady Steene had been ill for some years before she died. Her daughter had grown to hate the darkened room where her mother lay, querulous and complaining, with the continual smell of medicines and antiseptics.

Illness revolted Edith and she shrank from it; Helga's

obviously perfect health attracted her as much as her looks.

There was a vitality and strength about this young German girl such as she had never known before in any of the people she had met.

Even Cedric, her brother, the only person Edith really cared for in the household, gave no impression of good health.

He was good-looking, but he was too thin and his sallow complexion was accentuated by the manner in which he wore his hair long and dropping untidily over his forehead.

Cedric was a disappointment to his father for he took no interest in finance. Instead he was artistic in that he had a superficial dilettante appreciation of art without any real knowledge of it.

He idled through life making what his father considered to be the wrong friends and having among his immediate relations only one admirer, his young sister.

It was a strange household in which Helga found herself installed. Sir Alfred would leave the house immediately after breakfast and seldom return before dinnertime.

When he entertained it was usually in the form of bachelor parties of City acquaintances and it was the same at his house at Newmarket which he had recently bought, together with some first-class race horses.

Sir Alfred was always acquiring new possessions, yet when he had them they gave him little pleasure.

He liked money while he was making it, but what it could buy for him once it was acquired, was something which interested him not at all.

He had the true gambling spirit, the same joy of a man who sits at the green tables at Monte Carlo and is thrilled by the click of a roulette ball in a number.

The game is everything—the values of the plaques pushed towards him mean very little. It is the desire to win which counts, the joy of pitting wits and instinct against fortune.

The gambling instinct was the reason for what seemed to be Sir Alfred's amazing luck, which made men in the City speak of him as "golden-fingered Steene."

He would always take a chance and again and again fate favoured him. What had appeared as impossibilities to others became in his hands the advantages of fortune.

Often when he came back in the afternoon to Park Lane, Helga, entering the library unexpectedly, would find him sitting with closed eyes and drawn face, utterly exhausted, an untouched whisky-and-soda by his elbow, a burnt-out cigar between his long, thin fingers.

"I am sorry," she would say, retreating. "I had no idea you were in."

"Come in, my dear, come in," Sir Alfred would say wearily.

"You have had a hard day?" Helga would ask in her gentle, sympathetic voice.

"A hard day but a good one," Sir Alfred would answer as often as not.

Then at his memory of some triumph she could almost see the vitality flowing back into him, resuscitating and rejuvenating the whole man until in an amazing transformation all weariness was gone.

Sir Alfred, alive and pulsing with energy, was explaining to Helga how once again his intuition had served him faultlessly.

She understood very little of what he was trying to tell her. Finance was not a thing in which she was particularly interested, and the ramifications of Sir Alfred's business were too complicated for anyone, however efficient, to grasp quickly or comprehensively.

At the same time she felt that by listening to him, by sympathizing, and by trying to give understanding and sensible answers, she was in some way helping him and alleviating perhaps a little of his loneliness.

26

That he was lonely she had no doubt. Edith was too young, Cedric too hopelessly at variance with his father, for either of them to be his companions.

She often wondered to herself if Lady Steene had in any way been a companion to him. She thought it unlikely from what she had gathered from the household staff.

A woman racked by ill-health, dying slowly but inevitably through long-drawn-out years of pain, was not likely to be a helpmate to someone so dynamic as Sir Alfred.

He had loaded her with presents. Helga had been shown on one occasion a huge pile of velvet-lined boxes of jewellery which were to be kept in the safe for Edith until she was grown up; but presents lose their real value if they are not accompanied by affection.

Helga had the idea that Sir Alfred, at any rate during the last ten years of his married life, had cared very little for his wife.

It was curious how small an impression she had made on the vast house in which they had lived so long. Every room was stiffly arranged without any sign of a feminine touch.

Cedric's rooms alone had the stamp of individuality on them and that of a depressing and morbid character.

He liked mauve hangings and his books were all exquisitely bound in purple calf with gilt letterings. He disliked flowers and refused to have them anywhere near him.

But he had a cage of love-birds and a small blackfaced monkey who would not allow anyone in the household to touch him except his master.

After two years of being in almost daily contact with Cedric, Helga felt that she knew him even less than any chance acquaintance she might have made at a dinnerparty.

When he was killed in a motor-car accident she felt that she had in some way betrayed Sir Alfred in that she had been useless either as a friend or as a confidante to one member of his family.

Sir Alfred took his only son's death philosophically, but Edith was inconsolable, and it was only with great tact that Helga managed to make the girl discard her heavy mourning after nine months and prepare for her début into society as she was several months over eighteen.

Helga realized that to her many tasks was now to be added that of chaperone. She had many misgivings as to her ability to play the part to her own satisfaction.

That Sir Alfred and Edith would be pleased whatever she did was by this time assured, but she knew that once Edith was a débutante there must be changes and there must be some form of organized entertainment arranged for the girl.

It was amazing to her, even after three years, how few friends and acquaintances the Steenes had, in spite of Sir Alfred's money.

Edith knew very few girls of her own age and Helga had an almost insurmountable task in compiling a long enough list of guests to be invited to the coming-out dance.

She had bullied Sir Alfred into supplying her with the names of his friends who had sons and daughters, and she had taken the chance of inviting many of Edith's contemporaries with whom she had such a brief acquaintance that she risked being snubbed or the invitation ignored.

One thing Helga banked on and not without reason. Sir Alfred was well known to be a man of immense wealth, and Edith was now his only child and his heiress. But there was Edith to be considered.

The girl had undoubtedly improved in looks from the leggy, miserable child whom Helga had found crouched in front of a smoking schoolroom fire when Sir Alfred had first brought them together.

But her hair was lank and even the best *coiffeur* in

Bond Street could not prevent untidy wisps from loosing themselves in the most unbecoming way.

Clothes, however expensive, never seemed to fit perfectly on her too thin shoulders, or to hide her large, sharp-pointed elbows.

Helga would not have been herself if she had not realized that she was the worst possible comparison for Edith.

As the years passed she had grown prettier and a position of trust had given her a poise and a sense of security which had been lacking when she came, desperately in need of money, to England.

Strangely, there was not a suspicion of jealousy for Helga in Edith's feelings towards her; she adored her, all that she did she thought wonderful, and she was delighted for Helga to receive the admiration of everyone whom she met.

Nothing gave her more pleasure than to hear the German girl praised behind her back and to be able to run hot-foot with the compliment as one might lay an offering at a shrine.

She heaped her with presents and would have spent all her allowance in such a way had not Helga protested and on some occasions refused the gifts, even returning them to the shop.

It was pathetic in some ways, in others a blessing that Helga had come to the house, for otherwise this boundless passionate emotion might have been poured out on some undeserving object.

Helga was sufficiently wise to realize that sooner or later from such a situation complications might arise, and she worried as she wrote the envelopes and invitation cards for Edith's coming-out ball.

She had done nearly a hundred when the door opened and once again William, the footman, interrupted her.

"If you please, miss, there is a gentleman here. He

asked to see Sir Alfred and when I said he was out he said could he see Miss Edith."

"Miss Edith!" Helga echoed in surprise.

Edith had so few friends that it was something of an event for anyone to ask for her, either man or woman.

"Who is he?"

"He said his name is Mr. Swinton," William said. "He was sorry he hadn't a card."

"Mr. Swinton," Helga said, knitting her forehead in an effort of concentration. "I'm sure I don't know the name. You say he is a gentleman, William, not anyone selling anything?"

"Oh, no, miss, he looks a gentleman all right," William answered cheerfully.

"Well, I can't think who it is," Helga said. "Better show him in to me and I will see him first. Miss Edith will be down soon, anyway. If I want you to fetch her I will ring."

Very good, miss," said William with a grin, disappearing; a moment later he opened the door and announced:

"Mr. Frank Swinton."

He came slowly into the room. He wore a large red carnation in the buttonhole of his braided morning-coat and his black stock tie was flashily ornamented by a tiepin.

At thirty-one he would have passed anywhere for a decidedly handsome man. A moustache slightly curled at the ends covered the corners of his mouth and his dark hair was brushed back from his forehead and shone like silk.

He had the assurance and poise of someone who has learnt that confidence in oneself is more important than anything else in the world, and because of such confidence there is no need to fear the unexpected.

There was more than a suspicion of poverty about the patent leather of his boots, which shone, however, in spite of deeply engrained cracks in the leather, and a pin-point crease in his trousers made it difficult for any-one to notice that the cloth was shabby and practically threadbare.

It was at his face that Helga looked, as many women had done before her, and she found there a charm which was not entirely accounted for by what was ob-viously a desire to please and to be pleased.

There was something engaging about Frank's smile, about the somewhat inscrutable but nevertheless twink-ling expression of his eyes, and even in the deep lines under his eyes which deepened when he smiled.

Frank held out his hand.

"Are you Edith Steene?" he asked in a quiet deep voice.

Helga shook her head.

"I am Sir Alfred's secretary," she said, "and Miss Steene is in my care. I thought that perhaps you would tell me the reason for your visit."

Helga's engaging appearance took the formality from her words and Frank smiled as he replied:

"I asked originally for Sir Alfred."

"Yes, I know," Helga said. "Sir Alfred is in the City. He will be home this afternoon if you would care to call again."

They were still standing formally and Frank with a gesture indicated a chair and sofa by the fireplace.

"May I sit down?" he said. "Or am I keeping you from your work? I can tell you why I have come."

"But of course," Helga answered. "Forgive me."

She was a little flustered by Frank's self-confidence, he was so unlike the usual visitors to the house, and she could not quite make up her mind as to the true pur-pose of his visit.

Friends of Sir Alfred did not usually drop in casually, and Frank certainly bore no resemblance in any way to the business acquaintances that Sir Alfred interviewed at his home either by appointment or invitation.

Helga had grown used in the past years to dealing

with all sorts and types of people who came with saleable articles. Most of them preferred to wait for Sir Alfred, but a few of them tried to ingratiate themselves with his secretary.

None of them had ever asked for Edith, nor had they had quite the manner and appearance of this man.

She sat down stiffly on the wide velvet-upholstered sofa and waited for him to speak, but all the time her brain was speculating about him.

"Actually, I have come here," Frank said in a low voice, "on a mission that is one of sadness. Perhaps you can guess what it is? I was a friend of Cedric's, and it was only on my return to England last week that I heard of his death in an accident. It was a great shock to me."

"Cedric's friend!" Helga thought.

The idea had never entered her head. Cedric, like Edith, had made few friends to her knowledge, and certainly only a mere handful of them had ever come to the house.

They were mostly artistic youths of his own age who were of little interest to the other members of the household.

"Swinton," she thought. "Swinton. I don't remember the name."

But she knew that even if she had heard it, it would have conveyed nothing to her and would hardly have been likely to remain in her memory.

"Cedric's accident was a great shock," Helga said, "but he was killed instantaneously and he did not suffer at all."

"I can hardly believe it," Frank murmured. "He seemed so young to die."

"Yes," Helga said, "yes indeed."

There was a little pause and then Frank went on:

"I came not only to hear of him but also, of course, to offer my sympathy and condolences to his father and sister. I know how terribly they must feel his loss."

"Edith was certainly broken-hearted," Helga said. "I have only just persuaded her to give up her mourning as she is to come out next year."

"How Cedric loved her," Frank said. "He often talked of her."

"Did he?" Helga said, startled.

To hear that Cedric had discussed his sister with his friends portrayed quite a new aspect of his character.

"You sound surprised," Frank challenged.

"I am a little," Helga admitted. "Here at home he seemed to take so little interest in her."

She flushed and stopped, realizing that she was discussing the dead boy somewhat unfavourably with a complete stranger.

Frank saw her confusion.

"Go on," he said. "You mustn't mind telling me what you thought of him. I was very fond of Cedric indeed, but I think that even with one's best friends it is ridiculous to be blind to their shortcomings, don't you?"

"Was Cedric your best friend?" Helga asked, slightly incredulous.

This seemed like a dream. That this smartly-dressed, obvious man of the world should claim friendship at all with the morose dilettante Cedric was surprising when she thought of how he had apparently developed all the oriental side of his character, how he would often drift about his rooms in a dressing-gown until nearly luncheon-time.

Had she been truthful Helga would have said that in her opinion Cedric was incorrigibly lazy and that it was a fortunate chance he had been born rich enough to indulge in his lassitude.

This man who claimed his friendship had about him a vitality and strength of purpose entirely unlike anything she had found in Cedric.

Perhaps, she thought, she had misjudged the boy, perhaps he had been unhappy and she had allowed what had amounted almost to a dislike of him to blind her better judgment.

Impulsively she turned to Frank.

"You must forgive me for the surprise I have shown at your being Cedric's friend. In spite of living here in the house with him I knew him so very little."

"I cannot imagine anyone living in the same house with you and not wanting to know you better."

At the unexpected compliment Helga flushed and lowered her eyes.

"Perhaps I ought to apologize too," he went on. "He must have spoken of you and I have forgotten."

"There was no reason at all why he should have mentioned me," Helga answered.

"There we must disagree," Frank answered suavely, "for I see every reason."

Again Helga flushed and was at a loss for words until he said, "Won't you tell me your name and then it will perhaps awaken some very stupid and slumbering chord of memory."

"Helga Hildergard," she answered, and Frank putting his hand to his forehead said:

"Yes, I do remember the name Helga, but I am surprised; I am astounded. If you did not expect me to be Cedric's friend, to look as I do, can you imagine my astonishment at finding you?"

Helga got to her feet.

"I think, Mr. Swinton," she said, "you would like to see Edith."

"I am in no hurry," Frank said easily, rising also; as he spoke the door opened and Edith entered.

She was wearing a wide-brimmed straw hat chosen for her by Helga and encircled with yellow roses which matched the yellow ribbons on her chiffon-and-lace dress, and she was looking her very best.

"Aren't you ready, Helga?" she said. "You know we ordered the carriage for twelve."

Then as she caught sight of Frank,

34

"Oh, I am sorry," she said, "I didn't know you were busy."

"Come in, dear," Helga said. "I was just going to ask you to come down. This is Mr. Frank Swinton and he had come here to see you. He was a friend of Cedric."

Edith, who had stood indecisive until Helga's last words, came forward shyly with outstretched hand. At the mere mention of her brother's name her dark eyes filled with tears.

"You were a friend of his?" she said slowly.

"A very great friend," Frank answered, "and that is why I came to see you when I heard of his death just a few days ago."

"Only a few days ago!" Edith exclaimed in surprise.

"I have been abroad," Frank explained again.

Edith groped for her handkerchief which was tucked into her ribbon sash.

"It was all terrible," she said, her voice breaking on a sob.

"Please don't let me upset you," Frank said. "I wouldn't have come here if I thought I should make things worse for you."

"Oh, but you aren't," Edith said eagerly. "I am merely being stupid. I have wanted so much to talk of Cedric to his friends, and do you know you are the first, the very first, who has come back here since he died?

"When did you meet him?" she asked, "and how long had you known him? Do tell us, Mr. Swinton; you can't think how I have longed to know what he did when he was not at home."

"I met him first a long time ago," Frank said, "I can't remember exactly where, I think it must have been at some party given by a mutual friend, and after that we often met. He came to my flat and my club; we dined together sometimes and went to a theatre."

"But Cedric always said he hated the theatre," Helga interposed.

"Perhaps he and Mr. Swinton went to different ones, really clever plays," Edith said quickly.

"I admit that wasn't Cedric's choice," Frank said, "that was mine. I enjoy a good play, and even a good musical show."

"So do I," Edith said. "Helga and I often go, don't we?"

"Perhaps you will let me accompany you one evening," Frank said.

As if his remark transferred her thoughts from Cedric to herself Edith immediately relapsed into her usual shyness, glancing at Helga and murmuring an almost inaudible "Thank you."

It was Helga who broke the silence.

"Would you care to see Cedric's rooms?" she asked. "They have been left exactly as he had them and his books and pictures are all there."

"Thank you," Frank said, "I would like to very much."

Slowly the three of them climbed the stairs to the second floor. Here Sir Alfred occupied the front of the house while Cedric's rooms, adjoining each other, overlooked the flower-decorated countryard at the back.

Frank entered the rooms with the reverent, solemn air of one who walks into a church, while Edith moved with tear-blinked eyes. This was the first time Helga had been able to persuade her to see or touch anything which had been exclusively her brother's.

When she had made the suggestion of seeing the rooms she had thought how good it would be for Edith to break down in this way the miserable reserve with which she hedged round her unhappiness.

Even to Helga, the person she loved best in the world, she could not speak freely of Cedric because she knew, although the two girls had never discussed it, that Helga had little affection for the boy who was dead.

Now, finding herself moving freely in the rooms with Frank, touching the purple-bound books and looking at the many pictures which decorated the panelled walls, she felt a sudden surge of emotion.

It was as if she were freed of some chain which had held her imprisoned and numbed her by its bondage.

Her tears seemed less choking, less bitter, than they had in the months that were passed.

Cedric was dead, she would never see him again, but because her unhappiness was shared now by someone else who had loved him too she felt less lonely, less isolated.

No one else had cared, neither her father nor Helga and that had been bitter.

None of her brother's friends had written to her personally; Sir Alfred had received a few letters from Cedric's friends, but the majority of condolences had come from people who had written because they thought it good policy or common politeness.

Shy though she was, Edith had a sudden impulse to put her hand into Frank's, to stand, as it were, linked with him against the world who had misunderstood her brother, but she was incapable of doing anything of the sort.

She merely stood somewhat awkwardly in the centre of the room while Helga, acting as guide, showed Frank Cedric's possessions.

Only the love-birds and the monkey had gone, the former to the servants' hall where they were fed and looked after by the kitchen-maid, the monkey to the Zoo, where it had died after three months' misery in unfamiliar surroundings.

Edith spoke of it now abruptly.

"Kiki is dead," she said.

"Kiki?" Frank said.

"Cedric's monkey," Helga said. "It was always with him. Sir Alfred sent it to the Zoo, but I think it pined away."

"It died of a broken heart," Edith said. "It was cruel not to have kept it here."

She spoke bitterly, and for the first time Helga was aware how much Edith must have resented not being consulted when she and Sir Alfred had planned what should be done with Cedric's pets.

"Your father thought it was best," Helga said uncertainly.

Edith stared at her stormily across the room until Frank turned round to face her, saying gently:

"Perhaps the poor little beast is happier as it is. No one else could ever have taken his master's place."

Edith smiled at him through her tears.

"You do understand," she said, her voice hardly above a whisper, but he caught the words.

Slowly they descended the broad stairway. When they came to the first floor Frank pointed to the heavy mahogany doors which barred the ballroom.

"What magnificent doors," he said. "They lead, of course, to your reception-rooms."

Helga answered "Yes," and would have passed on but Edith opened the door.

"This is where I am going to have my ball," she said, "on the twenty-fifth, and you will come, won't you, Mr. Swinton?"

"I shall be honoured," Frank answered.

"Helga will send you an invitation; you won't forget him, Helga, will you?" Edith said almost eagerly.

Helga agreed, but her tone was not enthusiastic. For some reason, which she could not explain to herself, she was afraid.

She did not know why, but she felt a sudden mistrust of Frank. She could not help it, her tone became brisk and partly defensive when they reached the library again.

"I see you are writing out the invitations," Frank said. "Would you give me mine now? I am a little doubtful of my address in London during the next few weeks."

Helga sat down at the desk and picked up her pen.

Frank went on speaking.

"But I don't want to wait until the twenty-fifth before I see two such charming people again. May I be allowed to call, perhaps the day after tomorrow at teatime?"

Again Helga felt some strange misgiving within her, but before she could say anything Edith had answered softly:

"Please do, Mr. Swinton."

CHAPTER THREE

Frank sat waiting in Raoul's for Helga.

He had chosen a table which was discreetly veiled on one side by heavy plush curtains, and on the walls behind were prints of the Royal Family in gilt frames.

It was only a tiny place but the food was good and he thought it was unlikely that Helga would meet anyone there whom she knew.

Already it was past the hour when she should have been there and more than once he glanced at the grandfather clock which stood in the entrance-hall noisily ticking the minutes.

At first when he had invited her to meet him alone she had been afraid.

In the three years she had been in England working for Sir Alfred she had never once not been present at luncheon and dinner with Edith. She told Frank so.

"Then it is time you began," he said commandingly, and she had let him persuade her.

Now that she was late he doubted if she had had the courage to keep her promise.

Eagerly he watched the door for her entrance. He told himself that it was strange how anxious he was and how keen would be his disappointment if she did not arrive.

There had been many women in Frank's life, and

looking back over the last nine years since the eventful night of his mother's death, he wondered what would have happened to him if women had not found him attractive and had not in one way or another, because of their interest, fed, clothed, and housed him; Landladies who had waited without much hope for their rent when it was weeks overdue, women of uncertain age who had loved him madly and replenished his wardrobe when he had pawned everything except the clothes he wore.

Others of varying ages and circumstances, had all been unable to resist some charm in Frank which had developed more and more strongly as he had found it increasingly useful.

He had never regretted that blind, desperate impulse which, after his mother's death, had driven him from his home.

He had never gone back, but once when he was more despondent and lonely than he had ever been before, and when he did not know where to turn for help or food, he had spent his last pennies in going out to Kensal Green Cemetery on the chance that his mother might be buried there.

It had taken him some time, but eventually he had found her grave and had stood for a long while bareheaded beside the simple, cheap headstone which bore only her name and the date of her death.

He had wondered about her and what she would have thought if she could have seen him then.

Three years of independence had altered and hardened him. He had learnt much about the world, he had learnt bitterly, in a school where the weakest must go to the wall and only the strong survive.

He never thought of Emily and his father. He had always disliked his sister and despised the man who was responsible for the circumstances of his home.

Whether they were still living in Edward Street or had moved was a matter of complete indifference to him. He no longer thought of himself as part of a family

41

but as one individual battling his way through life, keeping his head through sheer determination.

Crystallizing within him was the purpose to succeed sooner or later, and by success he meant the gaining of security, and the possession of enough money to enable him to be his own master, to be beholden to no one.

That was all that he wanted: to be unafraid of the morrow, to face the future without anxiety.

From his earliest childhood poverty had made existence a misery because of what tomorrow might bring in debts and the inability to satisfy them.

And since he had been alone in the world he had known more times than he could remember when he had had nothing between himself and starvation save charm, his youth, and a desperate hope of finding a way out.

Frank had made friends in the underworld, but he found he had little in common with them.

It was in the bars and the dance-halls that he found it easiest to make an impression, to pick up odd jobs, or to persuade some woman who had more money than sense to take an interest in him.

All his encounters with the feminine sex, however, were not sordid.

There was one woman, the wife of a Harley Street specialist, whom he met when she was doing charity work in the East End.

She liked Frank, and, nearly his mother's age, it was only a maternal interest she had in the young man who, although threadbare and in need of nourishment, had obviously known better days.

She found him a temprary job as a secretary and advanced him money to buy new clothes and to rent for himself a small, inadequately lit, but respectable bedroom in Bloomsbury.

For a short time Frank was happy, then more and more he found the work irksome. It was far too much like the office life from which he had run away.

There were hours to be kept and routine to be observed and although at first the pay seemed princely after the months of living from hand to mouth, he soon found it was grievously inadequate when he had to keep up appearances again.

He was contemplating resigning the job, when the work came to an end and his services were no longer required.

It solved the problem for him, for he was doubtful if he would have had the courage after what he had been through to forsake an assured income, and he had not yet finished paying the doctor's wife for his clothes and her original advance for rent.

When he went round to see her to explain his position and also, to beg for further help, he found she had been taken ill, operated upon, and was not in a condition to receive either visitors or messages.

He deduced from this that fate did not intend him to trouble her further and he disappeared with the few assets she had been instrumental in providing him with.

More than once good luck came his way. On one occasion some young men who had much money and few brains took him, because he was good company, as their guest to Ostend, where they drank and gambled all night and raced all day.

Frank was wise enough to keep not only sober but awake to his opportunities, and he came back to London fifty pounds to the good and with a number of acquaintances who stood him in good stead for several months as providers of free meals.

By this time he had become an expert at turning any situation, however unlikely, to his own advantage, and he conceived the idea of visiting Cedric Steene's father.

He had never met the boy, but one of the men in the Ostend party had talked about him, and the accident which had resulted in his death, apparently due entirely to Cedric's own fault, had been cited as a warning to dangerous drivers.

"Funny chap, Steene," someone who had met him had commented. "My governor says that Sir Alfred is one of the richest men in the City today."

"Do you know him?" Frank asked curiously.

"Good heavens, no!" was the answer. "I don't think any of us are likely to meet 'Golden-fingered Steene', not socially I mean. But his son went to Eton and got sent down from Oxford after a couple of terms there. My mother wouldn't have him inside the house, needless to say."

"Who gets the old boy's money now?" someone else asked.

"I believe there's a daughter," the man who had known Cedric replied.

Frank stored the information in his mind, and later got the back copies of *The Times* and *Morning Post* and read the short descriptive articles which spoke of the accident and the death of Sir Alfred Steene's only son.

Sir Alfred's wife was dead, they informed him, and, as Frank already knew, he had one surviving child— a daughter, Edith.

Frank decided to call at the house in Park Lane. If Sir Alfred had been devoted to his son he would undoubtedly welcome a friend of his.

It is a weakness of people who have lost those they love in death to want to talk of them, and it would be almost impossible to prove that Frank had never known Cedric.

Who could tell, he thought, to what such an introduction to one of the richest men in the City might not lead?

After what he had heard he was pleasantly surprised both at the dignity of the house and by Edith. She was not at all bad, he considered, but when he thought of Helga his heart leapt.

How lovely she was, and how utterly unexpected to find someone like her in that great pompous library with its massive furniture and bound books locked in glass cases.

One would expect to encounter someone like Helga in the woods with the sun glinting on her golden hair, or in a garden where even the flowers could not rival the pink and white purity of her cheeks.

The very idea of her being a secretary was ridiculous. It was too prim and proper for the dimple, which could not be restrained, at the corner of her mouth, or for the sweep of her curling brown eyelashes which revealed her startlingly blue eyes.

It was, indeed, difficult for Frank to keep away from Park Lane after his first visit to Sir Alfred's home.

He called continually at all sorts of odd hours when he knew Sir Alfred would be in the City and there was every likelihood of Edith being engaged at the finishing classes which still took a great deal of her time.

Helga protested; she made a pathetic, ineffectual effort to refuse to see him.

But eventually she succumbed, as so many other women had, to Frank's charm, and welcomed him with a smile and eyes which could not quite conceal the pleasure she drew from his acquaintance.

It was nearly ten days before Frank finally met Sir Alfred and then it was Edith who introduced him as her special protégé.

Sir Alfred found him agreeable and, unlike some of the other young men who had come to the house, ready to listen admiringly to his talk of financial affairs.

Whether he approved of Frank's continual presence in his home there was no knowing. Sir Alfred was probably unaware that his visits were so numerous, and when he found him present at dinner he was quite prepared to be agreeable; he certainly made no protest.

Edith considered Frank her friend, and she had no idea that there were many occasions when he would spend an hour or so with Helga and leave the house without her even knowing of his visit.

Helga found herself driven into an intimacy of which she was afraid but which she could not control.

It was not possible for her to give the order that Frank was not to be admitted, and he was clever enough never to ask directly for her when he called, but to enquire of the servants who was at home.

The servants liked him and there was betting in the servants' hall as to which of the young ladies he was after.

They had known each other barely a fortnight when Frank, unable to stop himself, took Helga in his arms and kissed her one hot afternoon when she was waiting in the library for Edith to finish her music lesson before they took a drive to Ranelagh.

The blinds were lowered to keep out the sun, and Helga, when she had come downstairs, after a servant had announced Frank's arrival, in a simple dress of white muslin, seemed in the half light some beautiful spirit from another world.

She found him pacing up and down the room.

"You have been a long time," he said reproachfully.

"But I wasn't expecting you," she said in surprise.

"I know," he answered, "but I understood that you were going to Ranelagh at three o'clock. I will come with you if I may, but I wanted to see you alone first."

"Why?" Helga asked innocently. "Is anything the matter?"

Frank laughed; then he walked towards her.

"Do you really want to know why?" he asked.

There was something in his voice and in his eyes which made Helga speechless. She put out her hands quickly as if to save herself, but she was too late.

He took her in his arms and his mouth came down on hers desperately, as if he could not control himself any longer.

He held her tightly to him, crushing her with his arms until all resistance left her and he seemed utterly to possess her with his kiss.

46

When eventually he let her go she would have fallen had she not steadied herself against him, and when she could find no words with which to speak but could only raise her hands to her burning cheeks as though to hide them, Frank drew her close again.

"I love you, darling," he said. "Oh, Helga, you have driven me mad."

The clock struck three and they both looked at it with startled eyes.

"I must see you alone," he said.

"I can't," she answered, and her voice was very low and shaken.

"Tomorrow, then," he insisted. "You must lunch with me. Come to Raoul's at one o'clock."

"It is impossible!" she persisted, but he pleaded and commanded until she agreed.

They had only a few moments before Edith, who was invariably punctual, came into the room, already dressed for Ranelagh and carrying a lace sunshade.

She was so delighted that Frank was to accompany them that she forgot to notice that Helga was not ready and that immediately on her entrance she hurried from the room, averting her face.

The afternoon at Ranelagh was enjoyable, and if Helga was unnaturally quiet Edith was unusually talkative, laughing shyly at Frank's jokes and obviously pleased at being able to monopolize his attention.

Only twice did Frank manage to whisper to Helga when Edith was out of hearing.

Once he touched her hand, and his voice saying "My dear, my darling" brought the blood rushing to her face and made her lips tremble, and when he said good night he added,

"Tomorrow at one o'clock. You mustn't fail me."

It was, however, nearly ten past before Frank sprang to his feet as the door of Raoul's opened and Helga came in.

He hurried forward to greet her as she stood a little

uncertainly in the doorway. She was flustered and her eyes would not meet his as she seated herself at the table, drawing off her long kid gloves.

"Are you quite certain we shall not be seen?" she asked.

Frank reassured her.

"I said I had to go to the dentist," she went on, "and that this was the only appointment he could give me. It was all very difficult—never, never, have I had to tell so many lies. Naturally I was expected to take the carriage.

"Neither Edith nor the servants could understand why I preferred to walk. Oh dear, oh dear, I can't think why I let you persuade me."

"Shall I tell you?" Frank said gently, and when she looked at him she shook her head.

"No," she said, "don't tell me, you mustn't say it, not here at any rate."

"Why not?" Frank asked. "Are you afraid of loving someone? Is it so very strange?"

"It is for me," Helga said seriously; and she added quickly, "but I haven't said yet that I do love you. I mustn't, it is impossible, I have my work, I have to look after Edith, Sir Alfred relies on me."

Frank smiled tenderly, and talking her hand in his he raised it to his lips.

* * *

Helga leant out of her bedroom window which was high at the top of the house and commanded a vast view of the Park.

Through the leaves on the trees she could catch a glimmer of water silver in the moonlight, and there seemed to her to be a hush over London as if the great city were dreaming peacefully.

She felt that the whole world was waiting with her for some great drama to unveil itself. This was the overture, giving little indication of the tremendous events which were to come later.

"This is living," she told herself.

This transformation—not only of herself but of the world around her. All day she had felt as if that which was most familiar had altered and taken on a new aspect.

Now, when at last she was alone, when she could look out of her window on to his enchanted land, she felt that the emotions imprisoned within her must burst forth to illuminate her and all around her with some strange light.

This was life, when one's body was suffused with a feeling both languorous and thrilling, when one's eyes and mind found beauty in what was most commonplace, when one's heart was singing and the stars above were shining brighter because of it.

"I am twenty-five," Helga thought, "and I have never experienced this before."

From the moment that Frank had walked into the library that busy morning she had known, although she had fought against her thoughts, that he was to mean something unusual to her.

She had distrusted the feelings he had aroused in her, she had tried to avoid him, to dislike him. Before his lips had touched hers she had known that she was completely in his power whether he wished it or not.

But only now, with the realization of his love, would she admit to herself that she loved him.

The very thought of him made her a stranger to the girl and woman she had thought herself to be.

Helga had been a lonely child, for her father was often away from home and when he was not, much of his time was occupied with entertaining.

Like most of his countrymen he was fond of children and when he could be with his daughter he offered her not only the affection of a parent but the companionship and the undivided attention of one of the cleverest men of his generation.

He talked to her as he would to a grown-up person; at times he confided in her.

Although much of what he said was beyond her comprehension she strove, by her affection and by her interest, to show him how deeply she valued and looked forward to their hours together.

When he father was away Helga's life was one of serious domesticity combined with arduous tuition.

Teachers came to the house and the mornings and afternoons were allotted to music, languages, and those arts in which it was considered Helga, to be properly educated, should be proficient. But her education did not end there.

Although the house was large and many servants were employed she learnt to cook and to take her part in the still-room, which was under the sole charge of her aunt.

Jams, preserves, and cakes were made there by the ladies of the household, and although it was a task that Helga never regarded as particularly light or enjoyable, she knew that it was expected of her and did her work conscientiously.

There was always linen to be mended and embroidered besides the care of her own clothes, many of which were made at home.

It was a continual surprise to her when she came to England, to find that English girls were often completely ignorant of the things which every German girl considered of paramount importance.

How grateful she was later, when the crash came, that such a training had made her competent for the job offered to her by Sir Alfred.

The other lessons for which her father had paid highly efficient tutors were none of them so useful to her as the fact that she could tell the cook what was wrong with her savoury and could rebuke a lazy house-maid over an unmended towel.

In London she had attracted the attention of several important and eligible young bachelors, and if some of the English hostesses had been a little cold towards her in consequence it was not surprising.

"Don't be in a hurry to get married, my dear," her father had said to her in her first Season, but he need not have worried to warn Helga—she had no intention of rushing into matrimony.

She was enjoying herself wholeheartedly and with the eager enthusiasm of a very young child; and her emotions, fundamentally, were as yet quite undeveloped.

Her aunt and those around her always looked upon her as of an unusually placid character, but in reality Helga was one of those people who grow up slowly, and in girlhood her senses were untouched, the depths of her temperament unstirred.

Her father's sudden death and the subsequent discovery that an issue which he had recently made was unsound shattered the serenity of the little world in which she had lived.

Such a tragedy was too big, too overwhelming, for her to grasp anything save the fear for her future.

Her sensitiveness, moreover, made her dislike the thought of accepting kindness and what, in fact, would be charity from the people she had known all her life.

She fled to England, because of that country she had not only the happiest memories but also a profound conviction that the English, even those she had known, would not be particularly interested in her tragedy.

Three years was a long time, especially when one had severed completely every link and tie with the past, but now it seemed to her that even those three years were fading into insignificance beside this momentous present.

This was love.

Those vague, shadowy men she had once known who had whispered ardently into her ears at dances and begged her to listen to their pleadings—had they ever felt like this?

It seemed impossible, and she had dismissed them lightly, laughing at them when she was alone. It had all meant so little, and now, because it was Frank, meant so much.

She went over and over in her mind every moment of that hour they had spent together and the stolen minutes while they were waiting for Edith.

She thought of his eyes looking down into hers and the way his dark hair grew over his forehead and the feel of his hand as it touched her own. She could see him more vividly in her thoughts than if she had had a photograph beside her.

As she began to think of the household in which she now lived and played so important a part, Helga heard a quiet knock at the door.

Startled, she turned towards it, drawing her thin dressing-gown more closely about her. Who could it be at this hour?

"Come in," she said clearly.

The door opened, but for a moment she could not see who it was, for while she was silhouetted against the open window the door, which was at the other end of the room, was in a deep pool of darkness.

"Who is it?" she asked, and Edith came quietly into the room closing the door behind her.

"You are not asleep, are you, Helga?" she asked. "I am sorry if I am disturbing you, but it is so hot I can't sleep and I thought perhaps you wouldn't mind if I came up and talked to you for a little."

"Of course not," Helga answered. "Come in, darling. I wondered who it was."

"Why are you at the window?" Edith asked curiously.

"I was looking out at the moon," Helga said; "it is a perfect night."

Edith sat down on Helga's bed, curling her feet under her so that she looked like some small, dark pixy. Her hair was drawn back from her forehead and tied with a bow at the nape of her neck.

"Have you ever found your thoughts going round and round in your head so that you can't escape from them however much you try?" Edith asked.

Helga was surprised and hesitated before she answered.

It was unlike Edith to be confidential even with her, and she felt that if the child was worried or unhappy she must be exceedingly tactful or else Edith would never unburden herself.

"Yes," Helga said thoughtfully. "I think it happens to all of us at times, but it is worse when we are unhappy."

"It isn't because I'm unhappy," Edith said, still more surprisingly. "There's another reason."

Helga, who had been thinking that Edith was in one of her miseries over Cedric, climbed down from her seat on the window-sill and moving across to the bed sat down beside her.

She slipped her feet under the blue silk eiderdown.

"Tell me," she said coaxingly. "I hate talking in parables, or at any rate not coming straight to the point. What is worrying you, Edith?"

"Nothing is worrying me," Edith said with dignity, instantly becoming her reserved, shy self.

"I've frightened her," Helga thought, Annoyed with herself, at the same time feeling in her new mood as if she could not cope with anything that was not an outpouring and an outcome of joy and happiness.

There was silence between the two girls and then Edith said quite suddenly:

"Helga, why don't you like Frank Swinton?"

The question was so unexpected that Helga almost laughed.

'Not like Frank,' she thought. 'If Edith only knew!'

"But I do like him," she answered, trying to keep her voice casual, to prevent some new note in it from betraying her at the very mention of him. "What makes you think I don't, Edith?"

"You are so discouraging," Edith said. "You can see he wants to come here, to be invited to the house, but you always seem to give him the impression that he is not welcome."

"I am terribly sorry," Helga said. "I don't mean to appear like that."

"After all, he was Cedric's friend," Edith said hotly. "The only one, so far as I can make out, who cared for him. I want Daddy to invite him to the country next week. We are going down for the garden party and Daddy will ask him if you suggest it, you know he will."

"Do you think that Frank—Mr. Swinton—would come?" Helga said, protesting more to hide her own agitation than for any other reason.

A week in the country with Frank! Why hadn't she thought of it before? Sir Alfred's Newmarket home was open at this time not only for the racing parties but also for the annual garden fête which he gave for his neighbours and tenants.

Helga had already made the arrangements for the house party and for the fête. It was quite easy, she knew, to suggest one more guest, yet somehow the idea had never entered her mind.

"I am sure he would like to come," Edith was saying, "and anyhow I want Daddy to ask him."

There was a stubborn note in her voice which meant that Edith was determined, and Helga knew that even had she been against it the girl would somehow or other have got her own way.

"I will ask him tomorrow, I promise," Helga said. "It is a very good idea, I can't think why I didn't think of it before."

Edith got to her feet.

"Good night, Helga dear," she said gently.

Moving almost silently across the dark room she let herself out of the door without another word.

Only when she had finally gone and the first tumultuous excitement at the idea of Frank coming to Newmarket had subsided, did Edith's visit and its abrupt conclusion strike Helga as a little odd.

She had said that she could not sleep and that she wanted to talk, yet in all she had stayed only ten minutes.

For the first time a new thought and a strangely disturbing one came to Helga. Was there any other reason besides Cedric for Edith's interest in Frank?

CHAPTER FOUR

William was laying out Frank's clothes on the chair, placing a shoehorn beside the well-polished but worn brown shoes, and putting tie, handkerchief, and clean white collar ready on the dressing-table.

He was a tall, good-looking lad of nearly twenty-two, and had been in Sir Alfred's service already for nearly five years.

Frank watched him now as he moved about the room amazingly quietly for so tall a man, and then putting down the cup of tea he had been drinking:

"William," he said, "I have something to say to you."

"Yes, sir." William turned, all attention at once, a smile on his face which was, indeed, his habitual expression.

"I want your advice," Frank went on, speaking slowly as if he were choosing his words with care. "It may seem a funny thing to ask you, but I feel that you are a friend of mine and that I can trust you."

"Of course, sir," William said, "anything I can do."

"Well, it's like this," Frank said, lying back on the pillows. "This is the first time I have stayed here, but I have heard a certain amount about Sir Alfred's parties and I know a good deal about some of his friends. They are all very rich, William, and like all very rich men they like to gamble."

"That's true enough," William said. "There's a lot of money exchanges hands one way and another at these parties."

"So I have heard," said Frank, "and that's why I want you to help me, William."

"Me, sir?" William asked in surprise.

"Well, to use a racing term," Frank said. "you know the form. I don't. There was bridge last night, for instance. I went pretty slowly because I have to, but even so I came up to bed a loser, and, William, I tell you quite frankly I can't afford to lose.

"Now tomorrow morning I understand that we are going to see the gallops, and I rather gathered from the conversation that there will be a good deal of gambling done in a private and friendly way over Sir Alfred's new purchases.

"What I want, William, is a little inside information. If I win the gain will be yours too. We are sharing in this, but as I said to you before, I can't afford to lose."

Frank had spoken solemnly and seriously, but when he finished he smiled at the young man standing listening to him, and that smile seemed to touch some chord in William, for he grinned back.

There was at that moment an understanding between the two, a contact between man and man where each in himself was equal.

In half an hour Frank learnt more about Sir Alfred's friends and the inner workings of his stable than Sir Alfred himself was ever likely to know in a hundred years.

Frank was well satisfied with his morning's work before he sauntered downstairs at nearly ten o'clock for breakfast.

He had been told by Helga and Edith that no one was punctual in the country, but even so he was not surprised to find that he was almost the last.

Helga, of course, had had her breakfast at eight o'clock. She was in charge of all the arrangements of the household as well as the organization of the garden fête which was to take place that afternoon.

Fortunately it was a fine day and the sides of the great marquee already erected on the lawn were open.

Servants were carrying from the house plates and glasses and silver ornaments to be arranged on the long cloth-covered tables where the guests would find refreshments of every kind.

There was one other man having breakfast in the dining-room, a terse and at times somewhat truculent Canadian financier who, buried behind *The Times,* gave Frank a curt "Good morning" and continued to read.

Frank helped himself from the massive silver dishes which stood on the sideboard and poured out a cup of coffee. As he was seating himself at the table, Edith came in through the long french windows which led to the garden.

She was wearing a white blouse of *broderie anglaise* and a white lined skirt, and into her belt she had tucked two full-blown pink roses. In her hand she held a dark red carnation.

"I have been robbing the greenhouse for you," she said shyly to Frank, and gave him the carnation.

Frank thanked her and she sat down at his side to talk to him while he ate, but his presence seemed to make her tongue-tied.

It was Frank who did all the talking while Edith answered in monosyllables, watching him with her dark eyes, her thin fingers playing nervously with the roses at her waist until finally the petals spilt themselves untidily over her white skirt and on to the floor.

"Are you looking forward to the party this afternoon?" Frank asked her.

Edith shook her head.

"It is horrible," she said. "I hate it, but Daddy does it as a duty and every year we go through this farce of pretending that we like entertaining our neighbors and that they enjoy being our guests."

"But don't they?" Frank questioned.

"The important ones come only to criticize," Edith said scornfully, "while the others are pleased to come anywhere for entertainment and a free meal."

Frank looked at her in surprise. He had no idea she had such strong feelings, and he was startled by the note of bitterness in her voice.

Edith flushed as he looked at her.

"I am not criticizing Daddy," she said, "of course not. But when . . . I mean, if I have any money I shouldn't spend it on the people down here."

Before she could say any more Helga came into the room and Frank rose to his feet to wish her good morning.

He found it difficult to remember that anyone else existed when he was with Helga. She was naturally lovely, but her new inner happiness had brought her a radiance which made her appear to eclipse every person and everything around her.

Her eyes shone and when she spoke to Frank there was an irrepressible note of gladness in her voice, though her words were conventional and simple.

"How beautiful she is!" he thought.

Throughout the day her beauty continually thrilled him, so that he told himself again and again how wonderful she was.

Frank found it difficult not to follow her around as she moved among Sir Alfred's guests, talking to them, laughing, listening to them with that air of complete concentration which was one of her many charms.

Indeed wherever he was in the garden that afternoon he looked for her, striving for a glimpse if only of her broad-brimmed leghorn hat with its fluttering green ribbons.

Wentworth Hall was an ugly house built in the last years of the nineteenth century.

With pseudo oak beams, gabled windows, and un-weathered red bricks, its ugliness was only partially covered by a luxurious Virginia creeper.

The grounds, however, were magnificent, and the smooth green lawns and beds filled with a profusion of multi-coloured flowers led to shady shrubberies and woods where one could wander in seclusion for many miles.

After tea Frank felt that he could bear the crowds and the music of the red-uniformed band no longer, and he wandered away by himself after tactfully arranging for a small, chattering woman who had been boring him for the last half-hour to join in a game of croquet.

He walked for about ten minutes until the sound of music and voices was lost and there was only the rustle of the beeches and the chirp of small birds to disturb him.

Then he sat down under the trees and lying full-stretched began to think seriously about himself.

Where was all this leading to? For the first time in his life he found himself unable to plan ahead, content, for the moment, to drift with the tide which was carrying him along swiftly and easily.

When he had originally gone to Sir Alfred's house to claim an acquaintanceship with his dead son he had thought of it merely as an opportunity which presented itself with possibilities.

What those possibilities were he had not formulated but merely hoped that they would be immediately advantageous and have far-reaching results.

In the years of his life since he had lived by his wits Frank had learnt that the most unlikely events often turned out for the best, by which he meant to his advantage.

He had realized also that what mattered most in such a precarious existence was contact with other people.

Only through meeting people and making the opportunity to become friendly with them was there any chance of picking up information, money, or, as a last resource, work.

Anything might happen, Frank had thought, if he could gain Sir Alfred's interest.

What he had not anticipated was that his own interest would be aroused in someone like Helga to the exclusion of all else.

He liked women, he had liked them all his life, not only because they attracted him but because they cared for him, took pity on him, and thereby played a large part in his existence.

He was, indeed, incapable of talking to any woman, old or young, without flirting slightly with her and exerting, almost without effort, his charm to please her.

It would, of course, have been fulfilling his plan to be as charming to Sir Alfred's secretary as possible and to see that she wanted to be charming to him in return.

Yet from the moment he had started to talk to Helga, from the first day they had met, it became increasingly important to him what she thought and what she felt quite apart from her position in the household.

At first Frank tried to tell himself that it was because of her freshness and the fact that girls living such a sheltered life had not often come his way.

"It is the novelty," he said to himself, "it will soon wear off."

But even while he thought that he knew it was a lie.

There was already between Helga and himself some bond, some attraction deeper than could be accounted for by variety or environment.

When Frank slept he dreamed of Helga, when he woke he thought about her before actually his own precarious existence came to mind.

Frank had no real terror of the future. With the money he had managed to collect at Ostend he knew that if he were careful he could live for a considerable time.

He also saw quite plainly that his small nest-egg, combined with the position he had managed to forge for himself in Sir Alfred's household, could, if handled rightly, be the foundation of security in the future.

The question was—what did he want?

Always before when he had asked himself the same question in many different circumstances the answer had been—money; money, and escape from wherever he was at the moment.

Whether he was being looked after by some adoring woman, working at some temporary job, or merely existing on the charity of good-hearted landladies. Frank had always come quickly to the moment when he felt that he must leave and be once again his own master.

The desire and urge which had driven him from his parents' home and his job into an unknown and tumultuous world had kept its spur hard in him all these years.

"I must be free of this," he had said to himself again and again.

Now he did not want to be free, he only desired more of what was there, but how little or how much he was not sure.

"This is the life I have always dreamed of," Frank thought.

The same idea echoed in his mind as he sat that evening at dinner watching the light from the shaded candles reflect in the massive silver ornaments arranged on the dining-table, the shimmer of cut glass, the shining gold of Helga's hair.

The servants moved silently, handing what seemed to be an endless array of dishes with their white-gloved hands.

Frank suddenly had an insane desire to start a conversation with ...

"When I was in a doss-house in Bermondsey some time ago . . ."

He wondered what would happen if he did, how the company, so correct, so well dressed, would react. Only Helga, he felt, would understand; then he wondered if he were right in that assumption.

Why should she understand? What did she know of poverty, of starvation, or the ugliness and sadness of the lives of those people with whom he had lived?

The ladies left the room, the men sat down to a serious financial discussion until, with half-smoked cigars between their fingers, they had moved to the bridge tables. Frank won and was fortunate in that his partner, being old, wanted to go to bed early.

He could, at twelve o'clock, quite legitimately refuse another rubber and to to bed without risking his spoils of the evening.

Before he made his way upstairs he went into the garden for a final breath of air. It was a close, still night,

Far away in the woods an owl hooted and from the servants' quarters of the house there came faintly the sounds of a piano, otherwise all was at peace.

Frank walked across the lawns to the sunken gardens and turned to face the house. Only downstairs the rooms blazed with light, the upper floors were in darkness; from an open window he saw suddenly a slight movement and knew that someone was watching him.

He was quite certain who it was and something within him thrilled at the knowledge. Helga had called to Edith from that window earlier in the day.

She was there now, a shadowy, grey figure of which he could only vaguely discern the outline, but he knew it was Helga and he walked slowly until he stood beneath the window.

"Helga," he called softly.

For a moment there was no answer, as if she hesitated, then her head and shoulders appeared leaning out as she looked for him.

"How did you know it was me?" she asked.

"Shall I tell you?"

"Hush!" she whispered. "Someone will hear us."

"Then I will come up and tell you" he answered.

"No, no, you can't," she answered quickly.

"Why not?" Frank said defiantly, and without further words he went towards the house.

He entered through the garden door which led down a long passage into the hall.

Frank walked upstairs, bidding good night to a tired footman who was hurrying towards the drawing-room. From the first landing the wide staircase divided and led upwards to different sides of the house.

Swiftly Frank climbed the heavy-carpeted stairs. When he reached another landing he had no difficulty in guessing which of the three doors which faced him would lead into the room whose windows overlooked the front of the house.

He hesitated for a moment before he turned the handle. Would the door be locked? he wondered. Would Helga, frightened, or perhaps horrified, have barricaded herself against him?

He drew a deep breath, opened the door and went in.

It was dark. For a moment he had the startled thought that he had come to the wrong room, then a slight movement betrayed her.

He put out his arms, found her, and she yielded to him with a gentle sound that was half-sigh, half groan.

As his lips touched hers she tried to push him away. "No," she whispered, "no, darling, no."

Her resistance, the soft warmth of her body, and the fragrance of her, fired Frank with a sudden madness.

Fiercely, almost cruelly, he crushed her close to him, kissing her wildly on her face and neck . . .

He felt her response; knew that she too thrilled with an ecstasy and beauty beyond words, beyond reason.

"I love you . . . I want you . . . and you are mine . . . mine," Frank said hoarsely.

His kisses became more insistent, more demanding, then he lifted Helga up in his arms and carried her to the bed.

He laid her down then as he flung himself down beside her; his hands touched her body, his mouth holding her completely captive.

She gave a little cry.

"No Frank . . . please . . . you are hurting . . . me!"

It was a child's cry and Frank was still.

Then he said almost angrily.

"Do you think I would hurt you? My sweet, my precious love, this is different from anything I have ever felt before."

He laid his cheek against hers, holding her close against his head.

"Listen my darling you are everything I have longed for and never known—I worship you not only with my mind but with my heart and soul."

He felt Helga draw in her breath and then he said very quietly.

"One day—God knows when—but before we die—you will be my wife."

CHAPTER FIVE

William, brushing clothes in the pantry and whistling as he did so, watched through the open window as Frank set off for a walk with Helga and Edith on either side of him.

The whole party was leaving Newmarket for London in an hour, and Frank had taken the girls for a last walk before the car should arrive at the door ready to take them to the station.

It was a cloudy, gusty day and both Helga and Edith were wearing warm woollen jackets over serge skirts.

Frank was annoyed, as at the last moment before they set forth Edith had decided to come.

She was not fond of walking and he had hoped that the clouds which threatened rain would keep her indoors and that he would be able to snatch a quiet half-hour alone with Helga.

But Edith had quite firmly said that she thought the air would do her good, and it was part of Frank's and Helga's policy to encourage rather than in any way attempt to deter her from her purpose.

Perhaps it was a guilty conscience on their part which made them pay an increasing amount of attention to Edith these days.

When she was with them Frank, indeed, talked almost exclusively to her, while it seemed as if nothing was too difficult or arduous a task for Helga if it would bring Edith any pleasure.

Their visit to Newmarket had been prolonged from the Tuesday, when it was originally intended they should leave, until the following Monday.

The weather had been hot, and Sir Alfred suggested that they should not accompany him to London but wait until he returned to them on Friday.

This plan they had hailed with enthusiasm. The other members of the house-party dispersed and they were left alone, three young people, to enjoy each other's company.

A critical observer would perhaps have noticed the joy which seemed to radiate from Helga and have wondered what was the explanation of it.

But to the household which had known her so long, and in which she had always been a gay and contented personality, she did not seem in any way unusual.

To Frank, after that first night when she had lain in his arms, she grew dearer every moment. He had awakened early next morning afraid and apprehensive of what her reactions might be.

She had brought into his life something which he had never known before, something greater and more tremendous than he had ever anticipated, but for Helga, who had lived a sheltered life, he was afraid.

He had left her pure but at the same time his kisses had been those of a lover and their bodies had lain side by side.

Would she feel shocked and would she no longer trust him? He realized how innocent she was and how inexperienced.

When at last he saw her alone he realized for the first time that Helga was not merely a lovely and attractive woman but that she had character and a personality of her own.

That he should want her and she him was all that mattered.

In her happiness she was living every moment to the full, savouring every second of their companionship and of their intimacy.

There were, indeed, times when Frank felt that he should kneel at her feet, for she seemed so transfigured by her love that she became a woman glorified, imbued, as it were, with some greatness beyond his comprehension.

There was none of the shyness, the mock modesty, or the shrinking which was perhaps to be expected from her generation.

Instead she opened wide her arms to him, eager to give as she was to receive, wanting to pour out the flood of her love without reserve and without count of the cost.

To Frank she was a revelation in that her loving was so selfless even while she gave the whole of herself.

She made no demands upon him, she was neither possessive nor autocratic; every hour that they spent together seemed to draw them closer into a rapturous unity.

In public the only betrayal of their passion was their avoidance of each other's eyes and the difficulty they had of talking together in general conversation.

Edith benefited in that they flattered her with their attentions so that she was drawn out of her normal reserve to an unusal degree.

Apart from Frank's love for Helga, the visit had been a success. Sir Alfred showed obviously that he liked Frank and thought him a satisfactory companion for his daughter and his secretary.

His good manners, his deference towards the older men of the party, and his eagerness to make himself useful in any capacity, gained him the approbation of his host.

Financially, however, Frank's position was not good.

Thanks to William and the co-operation of the stable lad he had returned from the gallops the winner of a fifty-pound bet, but at bridge he had been almost continually unsuccessful.

He could not refuse to play for the high stakes that Sir Alfred's friends thought quite usual, and having neither their experience nor skill he lost rubber after rubber.

Luckily the bet enabled him to meet his debts, at the same time he was frightened at his losses. He realized that in this house there was no possibility of his refusing to meet a debt of honour or allowing it casually to escape his memory.

In their pastimes, at least, Sir Alfred's friends were strictly honourable, and Frank knew that the slightest sign of default would put him the wrong side of the front door quicker than anything else.

Quite apart from all that Helga meant to him now, he had no desire for this to happen.

For the first time in his life he was enjoying real luxury, not only in the evidences of wealth, as well-trained servants, valeting, good food and wine, and the comfort of the house, but in the whole atmosphere of security.

Here was something he had never known, and when Sir Alfred was away and there was not even the talk of finance to disrupt the charm of the gardens, it made Frank feel that he had stepped into a story-book.

He found himself dreaming childishly of a home in just such a setting where he could live with Helga as his wife and bring up a family in happy ignorance of the hustle, the vice, and the misery of big cities.

He could hardly envisage the future without Helga, and yet how she was to remain with him or he with her he had no idea.

He took off his cap as they walked along and felt the cool wind against his forehead. There was the firmness of the earth beneath their feet and the rustle of branches overhead.

"What a noise the pigeons are making," Edith said suddenly.

"The most contented sound in the world," Frank answered, "a pigeon making love."

He glanced at Helga as he spoke, but she was not looking at him but staring ahead, a faint smile at the corner of her mouth as from the happiness of her thoughts.

He could not be beside her, he thought, without the words "love" and "loving" coming to his mind. She looked so neat, so composed, her hair smooth and severe.

Could it be true that not so many hours ago he had crept into her room and murmured in that golden hair as it hung loose over her white shoulders?

With something like a start he realized that his thoughts had run away with him and that Edith was speaking.

". . . have you?" he heard her say.

"Have I what?" he said. "Do forgive me, I was thinking of something else."

"I said," Edith answered, hesitating now, obviously confused at his lack of attention, "have you ever been in love?"

She looked up at him and something in his face and in the dark eyes he turned towards her made her feel strange. But Frank answered her question easily enough.

"Of course I have," he said. "Haven't you?"

She shook her head, and as none of the three could think of anything else to say they walked on in silence.

When they eventually returned to within sight of the house Frank sighed.

"I hate to think I am leaving," he said. "I can't tell you how happy I have been this week. I wish the party wasn't over."

"So do I," Helga said gently, but so softly that only Frank heard her.

"You must come again," Edith said; "you must promise me to come again. As it happens I am sure

70

Daddy wants you to come the week after next. He was talking about it last night and saying that he had invited Sir Jasper and two or three other men and that Helga and I must arrange to be here. You will come, won't you?"

"I should like to," Frank answered.

The invitation was repeated later by Sir Alfred, who added, at Frank's acceptance:

"That's fixed then, but I expect we shall be seeing you before that, shan't we?"

Frank wondered a little why Sir Alfred was content to encourage him to come to his home without knowing more about him.

He could only imagine that the astute businessman chose his daughter's friends with less discrimination than when he engaged one of his office clerks, and with a lack of references that he would never have countenanced for a moment.

In that particular he was right for Sir Alfred had taken Frank at his face value and was content with that.

He did not know of a strange desire on Sir Alfred's part that his daughter should not choose her friends from among his business acquaintances or their families, for after nearly forty years in the City Sir Alfred had few illusions about his contemporaries, whether he called them friends or not.

* * *

Frank brushed his hair before the cracked and discoloured mirror.

It was perched on top of a chest of drawers which had once, many years ago, been painted white; now, battered, stained and handleless, it served him as a dressing-table.

The room was small and dark, the one window facing the back of another house, there being but a gap of ten or twelve feet between the two.

Lace curtains, torn and in need of washing, were draped modestly over the dirty-paned window, and it was only on a very bright day that Frank would be aware of sunshine in the world outside.

It had been Frank's home for nearly a year, and such is the adaptability of human nature that he had grown used to it.

There was little to recommend number 95 Albert Street except its proximity to the British Museum for those who were students, and the fact that his landlady was good-humoured and at times unusually generous where a nice-looking well-set-up lodger was concerned.

She was Irish, which accounted not only for much of the dirt and untidiness in the house but why Frank had once owed her seven weeks' rent without a hope of payment and without any real fear of being turned into the street.

Threats he received in plenty, but when he pleaded and promised, though both he and Mrs. O'Hara knew there was little chance of his fulfilling those promises, her kind heart—and perhaps Frank's irresistible charm—would leave him still in possession of the "second-floor back."

All Mrs. O'Hara's lodgers were gentlemen—at least according to her—for applications from ladies were not accepted.

They were a miscellaneous but masculine band who slept under the roof of number 95, which, with the rest of the house, was in need of repair.

There were generally two or three students and an Indian, assistant at one of the many Eastern curio shops of the neighbourhood.

One of the attics was rented by a waiter at a nearby café, while in the "first-floor front," the most expensive room in the house, lodged a chiropodist whose place of consultation was in a more fashionable street nearby.

They were not a prepossessing lot—though Mrs. O'Hara did not have to associate with them, for bed and

72

breakfast were all she provided—but her preference for Frank was partly because she firmly believed that he gave her house tone.

As she remarked to her neighbour next door, you couldn't deceive her where a gentleman was concerned, she knew one when she met him.

After Frank's successful visit to Ostend, when he could no longer stay with the friends he had made on that occasion, he came back to Mrs. O'Hara. It never occurred to him to take more expensive or more fashionable lodgings.

His room, of course, had been let to someone else while he was away and his few belongings had been stored in the basement in a cardboard box.

Frank had brought Mrs. O'Hara from Ostend a red plush pincushion trimmed with shells and a small framed view of the Plage.

She had been delighted with this and it hung on the wall of her kitchen downstairs to be pointed out proudly to visitors.

Frank's room having been let in his absence he inspected the bed with care on his return from Newmarket, for Mrs. O'Hara had at times been known to change her lodger but not the sheets.

The coarse cotton sheets could never in their pristine freshness have been very white, but on this occasion they were as clean as could be expected and Frank had gone to bed and slept peacefully until eight o'clock the next morning.

He had grown too used to hardship for the difference in his surroundings to keep him awake.

Before he dressed in the morning he polished his brown shoes, which still shone unusually brightly from the ministrations of the boot boy at Wentworth Hall.

They were new shoes, new for Frank, though they had seen some service before he became the owner of them.

When he had the money he was not so stupid as to

spend a comparatively large amount on going to a good bootmaker, although he knew that shoes were a most important asset where a well-turned-out man was concerned.

There were misfits to be found if one knew where to look, and Frank was already *persona grata* at a shop off the Strand which catered to actors with small salaries and gentlemen who were temporarily in distress.

It was lucky for him that his figure was stock size, for the suits which he had purchased in the same way had, with very small adjustments, fitted him perfectly, and it was difficult to believe that for a few pounds he had made himself look as if he patronized the best tailor in Savile Row.

On this windy, dark morning Frank finished his shoes, put them on, and with difficulty opened a stiff drawer in search of a clean shirt, for this evening he was going to see Helga.

He frowned as he saw that the laundry had not only torn the shirt in two places but that a button was missing from the front.

It was a consolation to realize that none of these discrepancies would show under his waistcoat but it was annoying, as the same shirt was to accompany him when he went down to Newmarket again tomorrow.

When he was ready he took his coat off the back of the chair and put it on carefully, arranging a white silk handkerchief in the breast pocket.

From a side pocket he took out another handkerchief which was unfortunately too dirty to be used again, and also threw away a bus ticket which he had used the day before.

He then patted his right breast to assure himself that the wallet which he carried there was safe. His hand, however, did not feel the accustomed bulk.

Hastily Frank opened his coat and looked at the inside. The pocket was empty.

For a moment he stared at his coat as though he could not believe his eyes, then he started to search almost wildly round the room.

He lifted the chair on which he had placed his clothes the night before; he dragged open the two top drawers in the dressing-table; shifted his hat, and his gloves,

He looked under the bed and on the washing-stand; there was not a sign of his note-case anywhere.

He stood still in the centre of the room and stared at his reflection in the looking-glass.

It surprised him to see that he looked very much as usual, a little worried perhaps, a frown on his brows, but not as a man ought to look who, from having what was to him a large fortune, had suddenly overnight become bankrupt.

He realized what had happened; his pocket had been picked.

There had been twenty-eight sovereigns wrapped flatly in a canvas bag and placed in a covering case of cheap brown leather.

It was, perhaps, unwise to have carried his fortune about on him, but he had been in a difficulty as to what to do with his money.

He had never owned a banking account and he had not felt inclined, with the money he had returned with from Ostend and which, after all, would not last forever, to enter into negotiations which would entail questions as to his address and maybe his occupation.

To leave anything with Mrs. O'Hara, even if it were locked up, would of course have been hopeless.

Of a naturally curious disposition Mrs. O'Hara never disguised the fact that she often looked through drawers and in the wardrobes when her lodgers were out, and she hardly bothered to make apologies if she was caught in the act by their sudden return.

She was more or less honest unless the rent was in arrears and she thought that her tenant had a store of money which he was keeping against an even worse predicament.

But the other inhabitants of the house had a code of their own. They were continually borrowing from each other and if one of them was out and a personal request for money could not be made they would certainly help themselves.

There was nothing left for Frank, therefore, but to carry the money about with him and he evolved a method of wrapping the coins in thin paper so that they should neither clink together nor make an unwieldy protuberance on his chest.

In his trouser pocket he carried his loose silver and coppers. He pulled his change out now and found that he possessed exactly twelve shillings and fourpence.

He remembered that he had changed sixpence aboard the bus last night to get home.

It had been a wet night, and the rain had been drizzling steadily the whole afternoon.

He had had a sandwich and a glass of beer at a bar where in the past he had frequently met a chance acquaintance.

But last night he had not been fortunate and having paid for his supper he had thought that an early night would do him no harm.

There had been quite a crowd waiting for the bus, everyone wanting to get a seat inside rather than face the rain on top.

Frank had pushed his way through the crowd of men and giggling women who were being assisted by their escorts on to the step. It must have been then, he thought, that someone with light but sure fingers had taken his case.

It would have been an easy thing to do in the crowd as he had elbowed his way under dripping umbrellas to the front.

He had not thought to look for his money when he

had finally got back to his bedroom and when he had gone to bed he had locked his door, so it could have been no one in the house, in fact there was no one to blame but himself.

When he had sought a place of security for his money the idea of pickpockets had never entered his head.

Thieves he had been prepared for, in this house and at Wentworth Hall. He had carried the money with him in the day-time and in the evening, at night he had slipped it under his pillow.

Self-reproach was not going to help him now; the money had gone and so far as he could see there was not a chance of immediately making any, unless the week-end at Wentworth Hall was unduly prolific.

Could he avoid the bridge tables? he wondered, and chance a side bet on the gallops? It was difficult to think of an excuse.

Sir Alfred expected all the men of his party to play bridge, and the numbers would probably be exactly right for two or three tables.

Should he not go? But in London his plight was even worse.

He had paid last week's rent but Mrs. O'Hara would expect another instalment tomorrow before he left, and if he did not give it to her he was not going to exist for long on twelve shillings.

Frank strode up and down the room trying in mental agony to find some solution to his problem.

There was no one to whom he could turn with his tragic story. Mrs. O'Hara would have swooned at the thought of any of her lodgers owning so vast a sum as twenty-eight pounds, let alone of having it in cash about their person.

Frank could well imagine Sir Alfred's scorn, after his surprise if he were told of a man carrying every penny he possessed about in his breast pocket.

With women such as Helga and Edith one did not discuss money.

The only person whom he thought he might make a confidant of was William.

One way or another William must help him when he got to Wentworth Hall, not merely with sympathy but with practical advice.

How could he carry on without money.

How? How?

CHAPTER SIX

By tea-time, when Frank arrived at Sir Alfred's house, he had already decided he must tell Helga of what had occurred.

He felt he could not possibly keep up a pretence to her that all was well with him, and that at any rate the strain under which he was suffering would certainly be evident during the week-end.

Helga, he thought, would give him sound advice.

Should he go to Sir Alfred and ask him for a job, or should he appeal to him as a friend of the dead Cedric and suggest a small loan until better times turned up?

He did not feel very confident about that; he felt certain that Sir Alfred, being the businessman he was, would dislike lending money. In the past he had often heard men of Sir Alfred's calibre, if not of his financial standing, remark, "My dear boy, I never lend money. I'd rather give it away."

He was wondering what excuse he could make to see Helga alone when the door opened and he found himself stepping into the hall and giving his hat and stick to the attendant footman.

He was shown upstairs to the small white boudoir leading out of the great drawing-room where the two girls generally sat in the afternoon. Compared to some of the other rooms in the house it was simply furnished.

Edith had her own room upstairs which had once been the schoolroom, while Helga was to be found at most hours of the day in the library, which she used for her work for Sir Alfred and as an office from which household affairs were organized.

The boudoir was a neutral meeting-ground where the small entertaining at present arranged for Edith took place.

Edith was sitting in the window-seat reading a book when Frank was announced and she looked up in surprise before she rose awkwardly to her feet and walked across the room to greet him.

It was extraordinary, Frank thought, how ungainly Edith was for a small woman.

Helga was head and shoulders taller and of far bigger build, yet every movement she made was graceful and rhythmic, while Edith seemed like some young colt which could not yet manage its long legs and, once standing, was surprised at its own ingenuity.

"How nice of you to come," Edith said conventionally.

There was a warmth in her voice which told Frank that her words were more than an idle expression.

"I didn't expect to be lucky enough to find you alone," he said with a smile.

He could not help making himself pleasant to any woman, however unattractive, even when his thoughts were elsewhere.

They sat down on the white sofa by the fireplace and almost immediately a butler and footman came into the room carrying a huge silver tray piled with tea things, cakes and sandwiches of many varieties.

In Sir Alfred's home there was what was known as a good table at every meal, a fact for which Frank had been sincerely grateful on many occasions in the past.

In spite of his troubles now he was ready to eat heartily for he had had no food of any sort since breakfast.

"All our plans are upset," Edith said, "and Helga and I are most annoyed about it."

"Why, what has happened?" Frank asked.

"You know our party at Newmarket tomorrow," Edith went on. "Well, Daddy decided this morning it was to be a bachelor one only. Some friend of his, I've forgotten who, was coming with his wife and now she is ill, and as that would make us eight men to two women Daddy thinks it better for Helga and me to remain behind.

"He is expecting you, of course, but we are furious at being thrown over like this."

"It is infuriating!" Frank said. "I was so looking forward to some more happy days at Wentworth Hall. Surely you can persuade your father to change his mind?"

While he talked Frank was wondering swiftly whether Sir Alfred would be easier or more difficult to tackle without a softening feminine influence.

Would it be better, perhaps, to see him tonight before he went to the country, or to wait until he was there before broaching such a difficult subject?

"Helga had to go down to Newmarket today," Edith said, "to make arrangements. She is coming back tonight, but not until very late."

Frank's heart sank; this was the last news he had anticipated. He felt desperately that he must ask Helga's advice before he acted.

She knew Sir Alfred and would understand the best way to approach him.

It would be ridiculous not to make use of her assistance, yet her absence this evening and the fact that it had previously been arranged that the whole house-party should travel down together at midday tomorrow was going to make it difficult for them to contrive a meeting.

"What time does she get back?" he asked casually.

He wondered if it would be possible to leave a note

for her asking her, whatever time of night she arrived in London, to meet him outside the house.

"I don't really know," Edith said vaguely, "some time after dinner, I think. Won't you stay and dine with me? I shall be alone, as Daddy sent a message from the City two hours ago that he had a business appointment and would not be back."

It was indicative of Sir Alfred's unconventional household that such an invitation should be lightly given and just as lightly accepted.

Lacking serious chaperonage Edith enjoyed far more licence than any of her contemporaries; and if on the other hand she did not enjoy their social advantages she was unaware of it.

Frank, feeling he could not stand his own company at the moment and glad of an invitation to a free meal, had no qualms about Edith's reputation and accepted with alacrity.

Perhaps he could wait and see Helga afterwards, he ruminated, at any rate he was not to have the opportunity of meeting Sir Alfred yet, whether he wished it or not.

Perhaps, after all, it would be better to wait until the week-end when there were certain to be a few minutes when he could see his host alone.

But his heart sank when he thought of the evenings at Wentworth Hall and realized that the assembled company of eight would make up exactly two tables of bridge.

In the meantime it was exceedingly important to stand well with Edith. He felt sure that the girl did like him, not merely for Cedric's sake but on his own account.

He was determined that, in the event of Sir Alfred's refusal to help and disapproval of his request, Edith's friendship must stand between him and a dismissal from the house.

When she could be persuaded to talk and discard her

habitual shyness Edith was not unintelligent, as Frank found now slightly to his surprise. Because he was being nice to her and they were alone she responded and laughed and joked.

Thinking of Edith as a person and not just as a shadow of Helga, he realized that, with the cruelty of fate, Helga, while befriending the girl, was a most unsuitable person to be with her.

It was impossible for anyone to find a personal attraction to the rich heiress while Helga was by her side, outshining her in every way, unconsciously but effectively.

Frank wondered to himself how long it would be before Edith saw this.

At the moment the girl was ingenuous enough to enjoy the admiration which Helga received, often far too plainly expressed by Sir Alfred's friends.

The deep mourning she had worn for her brother had prevented her from going anywhere, and it was for the winter months that Helga and Sir Alfred had planned a series of festivities, while her presentation at Court was to take place next year.

Already, although Edith did not know it, Sir Alfred had discussed with Helga the suitability of discreetly employing a chaperone with the correct social standing.

There were peeresses and other ladies of assured position who were prepared, for a not inconsiderable sum, to bring out a young girl with their own daughters and assure her of a London Season on the right scale.

Frank, laughing down now at Edith's flushed face and shining eyes, thought that after all the girl might have quite a good time if she could only make up her mind to enjoy herself.

Helga had told him how difficult she had been after Cedric's death and man-like he thought to himself that the others must have managed her badly to let her waste so many months in grieving over a brother who, from all accounts, was hardly worth it.

They still talked of Cedric, of course between themselves, but Frank and Edith found that there was really little to say about the young man once they had expressed how much they both missed him and how tragic his end had been.

It was strange that any man could reach the age of twenty-four and matter so little in the world.

Helga had told him frankly that she had not liked Cedric and he had sufficient preception to know that Sir Alfred had neither grief nor regrets for his son.

"If I died tonight," Frank thought, "I wonder how many people would remember me."

He remembered the past years; there were at least half a dozen women to whom he would be for many years to come a vivid memory.

He wondered how much Helga would mind, and, as usual, at the mere thought of her he found that his mind was wandering so that it was with an effort that he recalled his attention to Edith and what she was saying.

They decided that it would be ridiculous for Frank to go home and change for dinner, especially as Edith, thinking she would be alone, had ordered an early meal.

So Frank waited alone in the white boudoir while Edith changed from her afternoon dress into a simple tea-gown of shaded coral chiffon.

Chosen by Helga from one of the most expensive shops in Hanover Square, it was cleverly designed to flatter Edith's somewhat sallow complexion and show to their best advantage her dark hair and eyes.

Edith was childishly pleased at the thought of a *tête-à-tête* dinner with Frank, and when they sat at the great mahogany dining-table waited on by the butler and two footmen she found herself talking quite easily to him.

Frank, enjoying both the meal and excellent claret, told himself that by cementing his friendship with Edith he had done a really good afternoon's and evening's work.

Over a glass of port he half-thought of confiding in

her, wondering tentatively what her reactions would be, but she was too inexperienced, he decided.

Besides, were she to blurt out his circumstances to Sir Alfred with the mistaken idea of helping him it might make matters even more difficult.

Instead, he told her seriously how much the last weeks had meant to him and to what extent her companionship and that of Helga had brought him new happiness.

"I had forgotten how much there was in family life," he said. "I have known so little of it since my mother died."

"Tell me about your mother," Edith said.

Frank told her with a few embellishments the story of how he had run away from home the night of his mother's death.

"But what did you do?" Edith asked. "You had no money, no friends, and no work."

"Oh, I managed somehow," Frank said with a smile. "It has all been rather adventurous, but there have been moments of great loneliness when I have realized I hadn't a friend in the whole world, no one I could turn to in trouble."

After a pause he went on, "and that is why it makes me very happy and also very grateful, to know that I have a friend in you. It is true, isn't it, that you are my friend?"

"But you know I am . . . at least I want to be," Edith said.

Suddenly she asked, "If you've no money, how do you live now, if you don't work?"

Frank hesitated for a moment before he answered; he decided to tell the truth.

"I haven't got any money," he said. "I had a little to tide me over, but that's practically come to an end."

He poured himself out another glass of port from the decanter placed at his side, when the servants left the room and took a cigar after asking Edith's permission to smoke. She gave it absentmindedly; she was obviously thinking over what he had said to her.

"Where do you live?" she asked. "It's funny, but I was only thinking last night that we had known you all these weeks and we had no idea of your address."

"You wouldn't be likely to recognize it if I told you," Frank said. "It's certainly not a street that you or Helga are familiar with. Shall I say snobbishly that it's by the British Museum and leave it at that?"

"Is it a flat?" Edith asked.

Frank laughed, thinking of the tiny sordid little bedroom and the flickering uncovered gas-jet on the stairs which would light him up to it when he returned home that evening.

"It's what they call a 'gent's bed-and-breakfast'. Mrs. O'Hara, my landlady, is very proud of the term, but I doubt if any of your servants would view the room with much favour."

'I wonder if I'm being indiscreet,' he thought. 'Perhaps I'm telling her too much, yet what harm can it do?'

"But, Frank," Edith said, "don't you want a home of your own, a house or a place where you can have your own things, your own furniture and servants, where you can be comfortable and happy?"

"I can't think of anything I want more," Frank said, "and if you can tell me any method of getting them I shall be mightily obliged."

There was a moment's silence; then Edith, in a small, quiet voice, said:

"You could marry me."

Frank stared at Edith as if she had gone mad, then deliberately he put down his cigar and looked at her again.

She did not look at him, her eyes fixed on the dessert fork with which she was playing, pressing the silver prongs into the white table-cloth, making four tiny holes every time she did so.

"What did you say?" he asked; then without waiting

for her to answer he went on, "My dear, I don't think you know what you are saying ... that is if you are speaking seriously."

Frank could not believe that he had heard her aright.

The wild thought came to his mind that Edith was laughing at him, playing a joke on him, but it was so out of keeping with her demeanour that he knew he was not mistaken, she was seriously proposing marriage to him.

"I have thought about it for some time," Edith said in a voice that hardly rose above a whisper. "I somehow felt when you kept coming here it was not only because you were Cedric's friend, but because you were beginning to be fond of me."

Frank stiffened at her words but he said nothing.

"And then when you didn't say anything to me I began to think to myself that there might be some reason. I know perfectly well that people talk about me as Daddy's heiress and I suppose I shall be very rich one day when he dies.

"Helga and I have discussed men who are fortune-hunters and I know that nice men, the men one wants to marry, don't run after girls with money.

"That is why I asked you tonight how you lived, because I was quite certain that you hadn't got any money and I knew that because you hadn't got any you would never ask me, however much you loved me, to be your wife ..."

For the first time in his life Frank was utterly nonplussed. He was astounded at Edith's assumption that he had called day after day to see her.

While he had done his best to dissemble his love for Helga it had never entered his mind that the attention he paid to Edith would in any way be misconstrued by her into devotion or a secret adoration.

Now, however, he could see how easy it was for her, knowing so little of men, to misunderstand his flattery, his obvious compliments, and the efforts he had made to talk to her rather than to Helga when they were all three together.

But marriage with Edith had somehow never entered his head any more than he had contemplated it with any woman during the last nine years until he met Helga. Even though he knew she was everything he wanted in his wife, the possibility of him marrying her made the idea a fantasy rather than a reality.

How could he, in his particular circumstances, contemplate marriage?

Now he tried to think clearly and quickly, but the pause before he spoke, his surprise and hesitation, brought tears to Edith's eyes.

She sprang up, pushing back her chair so roughly that it fell over with a crash to the ground. She put a trembling hand against his breast.

"Why don't you answer me?" she stammered. "Am I wrong? Oh, Frank, oughtn't I to have said it?"

Only then did Frank realize that her question remained unanswered.

He got to his feet and took her in his arms, trying to find words to answer her, but she hid her face against his shoulder and he knew that she was crying. He held her tightly saying ineffectively again and again, "Don't cry, Edith, please don't cry."

But all the time he was thinking, trying to get things clear in his own mind.

With a little gasp in her voice Edith spoke his name—

"Frank," she said, "Frank."

Raising her tear-wet face to him she offered him her mouth with the confidence of a child who wants to be comforted.

Frank kissed her and she clung to him, with the desperate feeling of being caught in a trap that she had answered.

Upstairs, in the bright lights of the boudoir, Edith's

red eyes were painfully evident above a tremulous smile of happiness.

She held Frank's hand tightly and he tried not to think to himself how plain she looked. Her nose was flushed and emotion had made her more curiously pale than usual.

Frank felt that he himself must be looking rather strange and he wondered whether it would be possible for him to ask for a liqueur brandy.

"You haven't told me yet," Edith said at last, "not in words."

"Told you what?" Frank asked.

"That you love me," Edith answered.

"But of course I do, my dear," Frank replied.

He felt as he said the words that he betrayed Helga, and a sudden fear of her return made him glance anxiously at the clock.

They had dined at half-past seven but it was not yet a quarter to nine; supposing she came back earlier than she was expected and Edith blurted out in front of him the news that they loved each other and they were to be married.

Such a situation was impossible; he could not face Helga, could not see her expression and the pain he knew would be in her eyes, or listen to the insincerity of her congratulations. He must see her first, must tell her the news himself.

While he wondered wildly what to do the door opened; Edith dropped his hand and they waited for the footman to cross the room to give her a message.

"Miss Helga has just telephoned from Newmarket, miss," he said. "She is very sorry, but she had been delayed there and has missed the last train. She asked me to give you her love and say she would stay the night and would be up first thing in the morning, and will you please tell Sir Alfred when he gets back."

"A respite," Frank thought, and in his relief he asked for the brandy he had been wanting.

He waited until it had been brought to him, then after taking a large mouthful and letting it roll slowly down his tongue and throat he said to Edith:

"Listen, Edith dear, I must ask your father before you and I can decide anything definite. Supposing he refuses to allow our marriage, which he has every likelihood of doing. We don't want to be faced with having to make explanations to other people, however near and dear they may be."

"But Daddy will agree," Edith said contentedly. "I know he likes you and he wants me to be happy, I am sure of that."

"Even so," Frank protested, "he may not want me as a son-in-law."

"He will," Edith said seriously, "especially when I tell him how much we love each other. You will speak to him this week-end, won't you?"

Frank nodded, thinking what a different behest he had to make of Sir Alfred now to the small loan he had anticipated demanding of him.

"But until he replies," Frank said, "this must be a secret just between you and me."

"Mayn't I even tell Helga?" Edith asked.

"Certainly not." Frank's voice was sharpened by his anxiety. "This is our secret, our very own, and we mustn't share it with anyone until your father gives his consent."

Satisfied with his explanation Edith laid her head for a moment against his shoulder.

"Will you telephone me when Daddy says 'yes'?" she said.

Frank tried quickly to think of an evasion.

"I'll tell you what I'll do," he said. "I'll ask your father as soon as I can, it mayn't be too easy to get a moment alone with him, you know how occupied he is most of the time, and if he consents, I will come up to London as soon as I can to tell you."

"That will be lovely," Edith said with a sigh. "It

makes it all the more annoying that you are going alone for the week-end and that I shan't be there."

The idea of himself and Edith at Wentworth Hall with this desperate secret between them, and Helga at their side, would have been, in Frank's mind, an intolerable situation.

As it was he dare not think of going back to the house with its memories of Helga's love and of her surrender to him with the mission of asking for Edith's hand in marriage.

Quite suddenly he felt he could stand this no longer. Even now that there was no possibility of Helga's return he wanted to escape, to be alone, to think, to understand what had happened, and to what he had committed himself.

In spite of Edith's protests he insisted that he must go.

"Your father will getting home soon," he said. "It's better for him not to see us together tonight. I want you to sleep well, dear, and I want to think of the great honour you have done me."

He bent to kiss her hand. His words were inadequate and pompous, yet he was unable for the moment to say more.

Then as he felt Edith's arms round his neck and knew that she trembled because he touched her, he told himself he was a cad and that what he was doing now was worse than anything he had ever done in the past.

"She loves me," he thought, and wondered why, of all the women who had done so, Edith's love should make him feel ashamed.

With a desire to make amends he kissed her warmly, holding her tightly in his arms, so that it was with shining eyes and lips parted in happiness a few moments later she waved good-bye to him from the steps of the front door.

It was a warm night and Frank suddenly longed for the cold and roughness of the March wind which would blow away the mental cotton-wool with which he seemed to be enfolded.

Everything was unreal, the events of the last hours seemed to have chloroformed him into a kind of unconsciousness, and he wanted some stimulus, some crudity of ordinary life to awaken him again.

When he arrived at his lodgings and went into his room, locking himself in he sat for over an hour in front of the open window before finally he got wearily into bed.

In the morning he told Mrs. O'Hara that he did not expect to be back until Monday and that she could let his room if the opportunity arose.

He was awake very early and had played with the idea of going to Park Lane and making an effort to see Helga before he went down to Newmarket, but he did not dare to do so.

If she and Edith were together he knew perfectly well that the secret would be out long before he could find some way of breaking the news to her.

He contemplated sending her a note asking her to meet him outside, that it was a matter of life and death, and suddenly he realized that he was also afraid.

He dreaded the moment that he must tell her, he shrank from the agony he would cause her and the pain that he must suffer in telling her.

Noon found him at Liverpool Street and greeting, with a composure he was far from feeling, the other members of Sir Alfred's house party with whom he was acquainted.

Sir Alfred did his parties in style. There was no question of his guests buying their own tickets or being forced to provide food for the journey; everything was arranged.

Servants met them at the station with first-class tickets and a cold luncheon was laid out in a private coach where they were waited on by Sir Alfred's butler and footmen.

It was lucky that these arrangements were made, Frank thought a little grimly, as he tipped the porter sixpence who carried his bag to the coach. He had managed his luggage himself until he reached the station.

Then, appearances must be kept up and he must stroll nonchalantly on to the platform as if he had not sat on the top of a bus for the last half-hour nursing a heavy Gladstone bag on his knee.

Three of the party he had met casually at one of Sir Alfred's dinner parties, one of the men had been present the week-end before; the other three were strangers.

The time for the departure of the train grew nearer, but there was still no sign of Sir Alfred, and just as they were all becoming anxious an office messenger came running down the platform and spoke to the butler.

"Sir Alfred is very sorry, gentlemen," he said to them a minute or so later, "but owing to the pressure of business he is unable to catch this train. He will follow on later and will you please ask for everything you want."

It would have been difficult over luncheon to have thought of anything that was not provided.

Patties of every variety, cold meats, and hot-house fruits were served with an excellent burgundy, while there was also a variety of liqueurs, cigars, and hot coffee.

"I shall always be travelling like this in the future," Frank could not help thinking to himself.

He looked at his fellow travellers, corpulent, well-fed men, their waistcoats ornamented with large gold watch-chains, holding at one end no doubt a well-filled sovereign-case to balance an expensive gold hunter at the other.

He wondered what they would say if he told them that the few shillings in his pocket was the only money that he possessed in the world.

He had a sudden picture of himself, hat in hand,

making a collection, and he wondered what would be the amount contributed.

They were polite to him, of course, but he knew that were they to realize on what mission he was going to Newmarket, and that there was a likelihood of his being Sir Alfred's son-in-law, their smiles would be doubled in intensity and their geniality very near fawning.

"The power of money, the power of money, the power of money"—the wheels of the train seemed to repeat the words over and over again.

"What is the use of fighting?" Frank asked. One could not escape from it.

He watched his mother driven to death by the same Juggernaut. "We can't afford it"—those awful words which had coloured his childhood.

Even now he sometimes heard her voice in his dreams and more vivid to his memory than anything he himself had ever possessed was her worn black leather purse with its empty, gaping pockets.

As soon as luncheon was cleared away cards were brought. Utterly reckless, spurred on by some madness in himself, Frank over-called, laughed at high stakes, and in the perversity of fate won every trick.

He held phenomenal hands, he played brilliantly, and because it did not matter, because nothing could save him now from the fate to which the train was carrying him nearer mile by mile.

He had won ten pounds before the rubber was finished and they began to collect their things together for the next stop, Newmarket.

* * *

Frank went up early to dress for dinner. He wanted to escape from the company of the other guests.

He was tired of their chatter of finance, the smutty stories they told with guffaws of laughter, the smell of their big cigars, and the references, thinly veiled, which they made to the wealth of their host.

It was obvious that most of them envied Sir Alfred his possessions and that their friendship for him was entirely on a cash basis.

The men meant well, they were all good fellows in their own way, yet Frank felt a sudden loathing of their hypocrisy.

It was with difficulty he checked himself from saying how much he admired Sir Alfred and how, in his eyes anyway, the financier's value lay in his strength and tenacity as much as in his banking account.

He knew that the conversation would be very different in his presence once he became Sir Alfred's son-in-law.

Then bitterly he asked himself if he had any right to criticize; wasn't he intending to benefit himself by Sir Alfred's money?

His thoughts were chaotic, his feelings tempestuous, and as he closed the library door behind him he almost ran upstairs to the solitude and quiet of his bedroom.

Once there he put his elbows on the window-sill and stared out into the garden, seeing—not the green lawns and colourful flower-beds, but rather a panorama of his whole life up to this moment.

The real reason for his discontent, his unhappiness and indecision, he knew he was in fact due to one person, Helga.

He could not escape the thought of her and he found himself saying out aloud:

"I can't do it, I can't!"

There was a knock on his door.

Without turning his head he said "Come in," thinking it was the footman come to put out his clothes or with a can of hot water.

He heard the door open and close again; he was aware that someone was in the room, waiting for him to turn round, was conscious with a strange intensity of someone standing still and waiting.

Helga was facing him. She was very pale and her eyes, looking straight at him, seemed unnaturally large.

She wore a dress of some dark, thin material which made her appear older, or was it perhaps that some radiance had gone from her face, leaving there instead a look of anxiety and unhappiness?

"Helga!" Frank ejaculated.

He was so surprised at seeing her that for the moment he could think of nothing to say; then as he met her eyes he was aware that she knew everything.

For seconds that seemed interminable they faced each other, until finally Frank, afraid of the silence, afraid of the tension between them, spoke again.

"Why are you here?" he said.

His commonplace question seemed to break some spell which enveloped her; it shattered her stillness, and she moved towards him as she answered in a low voice:

"I came down with Sir Alfred. He had work to do in the train."

She came slowly nearer until she was beside him, her face raised to his.

Almost roughly Frank said "You know, don't you?"

Helen nodded her head "Sir Alfred told me," she said.

Frank could hear in her voice and see in her face that she was suffering from shock. At the moment she appeared almost numbed with the pain of this knowledge.

"Oh, my darling, my sweet!" he cried. "What am I to do? Help me . . . tell me."

He put out his arms to touch her and as he did so something seemed to break within him; he fell on his knees beside her, his head buried against her, his arms around her waist.

Wildly, blindly, stumbling over his words. letting them fall from him in a hoarse incoherence, he tried to tell her what had occurred.

He felt the flood tide of his misery pour itself out; his voice died away into a silence filled with emotion.

Her hand touched his head and he heard in the depths of his despair her voice murmuring his name again and again.

"What am I to do, what am I to do, my precious?" he asked.

Raising his face he saw that great tears were trickling down her cheeks. Unsteadily he rose to his feet and took her in his arms, and for a long moment they stood together, holding desperately to each other as two children might who are lost.

There was no passion in their embrace, only agony and fear. Finally Helga moved gently in his arms and taking a handkerchief from her belt wiped her eyes.

She turned away from him, looking out of the window, and he knew that she was fighting for composure, preventing herself from giving way as he had done.

"I can't do it," Frank said, "I can't! Come away with me now, Helga, we will manage somehow. I'll find a job . . . we'll get married . . ."

Even as he spoke the words he knew they were mere bravado. What hope had they? What chance? He felt his words were useless, without conviction and without any strength of purpose.

"Edith is very, very happy," Helga whispered.

"My God!" He could say no more.

He stood looking at Helga's back, at the firm proud shoulders, the long graceful neck, at the plait of hair with its gleaming golden tones, so dear, so beloved, every inch of her a part of him, every movement and every breath bewitching and compelling him to love her more.

He wanted to cry out, to seize her and rush from the house, to take her and make her his.

He clenched his hands against his sides, and as he did so the faint jingle of silver in his pocket reminded him how little there was between him and starvation. Fate had ensnared them both, there was no hope, no chance of escape or of reprieve.

"Will you forgive me?" he asked, his voice very humble.

Helga turned to face him and for the first time since she had come into the room she smiled, and it was the tender, gentle smile of a mother for a beloved child.

"There is nothing to forgive," she said. "I understand—oh, my darling, do believe that I understand completely."

"I came to see you, I had no idea, no thought of anything else," Frank said.

"I know," she answered, "Edith told me but now it's done."

"But Sir Alfred?" Frank stammered. "Surely—"

"Sir Alfred is quite pleased," she interrupted. "Edith has always been a problem to him, he wants to see her settled. Apart from that, anything she has set her heart on he is prepared to give her."

The clock outside on the landing struck the half-hour.

"I must go," Helga said, and her voice broke on the words.

They stared at each other, then Frank caught her to him, crushing her in his arms, bruising her with his violence.

"I love you," he said again and again, "I love you, and I haven't the courage to take you and make you belong to me. I am a coward, Helga, but, oh God, how I love you!"

He kissed her almost brutally until the blood came flooding into her cheeks and she lay breathing tumultuously in his arms. As suddenly as he had seized her, Frank let her go.

He almost threw her from him, turning away and pressing his hands to his temples.

"Go now," he said, "go quickly for Christ's sake. I can't stand any more."

There was the soft rustle of her skirts, the turning of the door handle, the dull hollow sound of a closing door, and he knew that he was alone.

For a long time he stood staring blindly out into the garden before he turned to face an empty room.

How Frank managed to get through dinner he had no idea. He could eat nothing, sending dish after dish away untasted, and although he drank heavily, alcohol seemed to have no effect except to make his despair more profound, his depression more intense.

Once or twice he caught Sir Alfred's eye upon him and realized with cynical humour that his behaviour was being attributed to nervousness and anxiety about their coming interview.

"He thinks I'm afraid he may turn me down as a son-in-law," Frank thought and wished that would happen.

If Sir Alfred refused to allow him to marry Edith perhaps he could then ask for a job, a job which, if it were secure, would make possible marriage with Helga.

For the first time since he left home nine years ago Frank found himself missing the security of office life, and that safe job he had held when he was twenty-two. By now he might have been earning five or six pounds a week. But he knew he would never have kept the post, such a life was utterly incompatible to him.

He might be a ne'er-do-well, a roving scamp, even a "bad lot"—they were all adjectives which had been applied to him at one time or another during his life—yet he had tried to live, not merely stagnate.

He could not imagine himself a respectable office clerk, any more than he could imagine Helga loving such a man.

He was recalled from his dreams to find the footman at his elbow with coffee.

He helped himself automatically; the thin Sèvres china cup encased in a silver holder, the huge crested silver tray and ornate coffee-pots made him realize once again his position.

99

With all the money he possessed in his pocket he was about to ask one of the richest men in England for the hand of his daughter in marriage.

Quite suddenly the humour of the situation struck him. If he loved Edith there would be some justification for his presumption, but he did not, he hadn't even a deep affection or friendship for her.

She wanted him, that was the point, and like the toys she had desired in childhood and the frills and furbelows she had coveted in girlhood he was to be bought.

His sense of humility vanished; he felt that whatever happened he would not feel himself beholden to Sir Alfred and his daughter.

They wanted him for himself just as much as he wanted their money; very well, it was a straight bargain.

His love for Helga, his desire and need for her, was the price he was going to pay, and it was a big one.

She was to him everything that mattered, not only in her lovely and loving self but in that she was the personification of all his ideals of happiness and beauty.

This evening in his bedroom he had said good-bye to her as surely as if he were never to see her again.

Between them now was growing every moment a higher barrier; it would be impossible in the future even for them to be great friends; honour, self-respect, and decency would keep them apart.

At that moment Frank saw his life stretching down through the years as a long grey road, empty, lonely, and cheerless because Helga was not with him.

Resolutely he turned away from such a picture. Deliberately he saw himself instead with money and with influence, taking his position in the social world, having, for the first time in his life, horses, cars, clubs, possessions.

In was difficult to visualize, and still more difficult to remember that always by his side would be Edith.

What was she really like, he wondered, this girl he was going to marry?

He knew so little about her, had been so little interested in her that he could hardly recall a conversation with her or remember any one of her likes or dislikes.

He remembered Helga once saying to him:

"Edith is a strange person. She gets ideas into her head and nothing one can say or do will alter them. She is fond of me, and I have tried so hard to understand her and yet at times I think I have failed utterly."

Frank thought of Helga's words now and remembered too that he had listened to them not because he was interested in Edith but because everything Helga said was important to him.

"A dark, awkward girl, unimportant and unattractive," would have been Frank's summing up of Edith in the early days of their acquaintance.

It was strange how unlike she was to her father, for Sir Alfred had undoubtedly a charm of manner and a vitality which made it impossible for people to ignore his presence.

As they rose to leave the dining-room Sir Alfred put a hand on Frank's arm.

"I understand you want to have a word with me, young man," he said. "Better come to my study in a quarter of an hour or so. I have got a telephone-call to put through to London first."

While the other guests chattered and talked Frank walked restlessly out on to the terrace through the open windows of the dining-room, feeling apprehensive and nervous even while he scoffed at himself for being so.

"This is a great moment in my life," he told himself. "I have come to the cross-roads, a secure future is in front of me."

But he felt no elation.

Three times in as many minutes he walked back to the window to look at the time. Savagely he hurled his partly smoked cigar away into the darkness of the garden.

It was quiet and cool under the trees. Frank moved

across the lawn, hearing only the distant hoot of an owl and the shrill whistle of the bats as they swirled their way against the star-strewn sky.

He felt as if he were waiting for some verdict; such a feeling was ridiculous, he knew; of course Sir Alfred would give his consent, yet some inner sense assured him that he was not mistaken ... he was waiting.

Slowly he walked back to the house and going in through the garden door went to Sir Alfred's study. He hesitated for a moment outside, then turned the handle and went in.

Sir Alfred was sitting at his desk with several papers in front of him, the telephone at his side, and in his hand a letter.

He read it; then rising to his feet he walked over to the fireplace.

"I have had bad news," he said to Frank, "very bad news."

"I am sorry to hear that," Frank said.

"I think you will be sorry too," Sir Alfred said. "It is about Helga."

Frank stiffened; an icy hand seemed to grasp his heart.

"What is it?" he asked, hardly above a whisper.

"She left a note for me before she went back to London," Sir Alfred said. "I have just been reading it. She has had an urgent message from her relations in Germany and without saying good-bye, without even giving me time to help, she has gone to Berlin. I don't understand it."

There was silence.

"We shall miss her, we shall miss her very much," he said after a moment.

And Frank, the blood thundering in his ears, heard his own voice say:

"Yes, sir, we shall miss her—very much."

CHAPTER SEVEN

Frank took up the picture paper and propped it in front of him on the breakfast-table.

"Anything interesting in the paper?" he asked Edith, sitting opposite him.

She had been downstairs some time before he had appeared, for she liked to see her father before he left for the office and while he breakfasted was her opportunity.

"You will find it interesting, I dare say," Edith answered.

After three months of married life Frank knew by the tone of her voice that something had upset her.

He looked at the paper, wondering what Edith was referring to. On the front page was the smiling face of an attractive American actress whom they had become acquainted with on their honeymoon in Rome.

All too well he recalled the scenes and sulks in which Edith had indulged because he happened to remark that he considered her amusing and pretty.

Now the newspaper's announcement that she had arrived in London filled him with gloomy forebodings that once again he was to be subjected to Edith's insatiable jealously.

He did not speak for a moment but Edith, having seen that he recognized the picture, continued:

"I can't think how you admire such a common type, it is quite obvious that her hair is dyed, but then I suppose men are stupid about things like that—any woman would know at once."

"I'm afraid I'm not interested one way or another," Frank remarked.

"But you were, weren't you?" Edith persisted. "Why, that first night we saw her at the Excelsior you could hardly take your eyes off her."

"Must we go over all that again?" Frank asked wearily. "I told you at the time and I've told you a thousand times since that I am not interested in this woman or ever likely to be.

"You asked me if I thought she was pretty, I told you that I did, and on the one occasion that we met her I thought she was quite amusing. Surely that's not going to be dragged up for the rest of our lives."

"It's not so much what you've said," Edith answered hotly, "as what you feel about her. I've not forgotten the way you looked."

"Oh, for heaven's sake drop the subject!" Frank said, throwing the paper on the floor. "I am sick and tired of it! Anyone would think I'd spent a night with the woman instead of being, at the outside, twenty minutes in her company."

Edith sprang to her feet.

"Really, Frank," she said, "I think you are disgusting. You say these sort of things merely to hurt and humiliate me."

She rushed out of the room, slamming the door behind her. Frank sighed and, helping himself to toast and marmalade, continued his breakfast. He was not perturbed by Edith's outburst, only bored to a state almost of exasperation.

He had learnt from bitter experience in the last three months that Edith enjoyed these scenes, they gave her some outlet which her strange nature craved.

She would cry now alone for some time in her room;

then she would seek him out and flinging her arms about him would entreat him to forgive her and to tell her again and again how much he loved her.

She would squeeze all the drama and emotion that were possible out of the situation.

She appeared to enjoy humiliating herself; it would be an hour or so before she was finally pacified from tears to smiles, before she could be certain of her faith in his love, and before she would let them return to normal life.

The honeymoon, spent in Italy at Rome, Florence, and Venice, had cost Sir Alfred a large sum, but it had made neither of them happy.

Frank could not help being haunted by the thought of how much he would have enjoyed the luxury hotels, the sight-seeing and the beauty of everything had he been with almost any other companion.

They had been married five weeks after Frank's interview with Sir Alfred at Newmarket.

There was no reason for waiting, Edith was in a rapturous state of delight at the announcement of her engagement, it was the end of the summer and Sir Alfred wished to leave London to go abroad.

With Helga gone Edith took over the management of the house. Though she flattered herself that she was succeeding admirably, Sir Alfred and Frank were continually conscious of how much they missed Helga.

Without her calm efficiency things were not the same, the house in Park Lane was reverting to its previous state.

Sir Alfred decided that Edith and Frank should live with him when they were married, and Frank, having no wish to start married life with Edith in some new home of her choosing, agreed.

Their wedding was quiet. Frank determined that at all costs he must avoid publicity.

He had two reasons for wanting to do so: the fear that even now after nine years his father and sister might seek him out; and the knowledge of what Sir Alfred's acquaintances would say of the marriage.

That he would be called a fortune-hunter was inevitable, but he felt he could face it better when he was firmly established in the house as Edith's husband, when they were actually man and wife and no amount of gossip, however spiteful, could alter the fact.

To his relief both Edith and Sir Alfred agreed with him, Edith from shyness and Sir Alfred because without Helga he felt he could not cope with a large social ceremony.

From Helga there was no news of any sort. Frank hoped day after day almost to desperation that she would relent and return, even while he knew that the situation if she did would be intolerable.

Although Sir Alfred talked about her constantly, every time her name was mentioned Frank felt a sudden throbbing of his heart.

The knowledge that he had lost her, that she had gone from him forever, was agony.

Once Edith said to him:

"Are you glad Helga isn't here?"

"Why glad?" he asked cautiously, wondering what she had in her mind.

"We shouldn't have been alone so much," Edith answered. "You liked Helga, didn't you, Frank?"

"She was very nice," he said calmly.

He had grown weary of Edith's probing questions; they were usually followed by a scene.

"But you like having me alone, don't you?" Edith persisted.

"Of course," Frank replied. "Of course."

He could bear the conversation no longer and had risen suddenly to his feet.

"I want to get something," he said abruptly and he was gone from the room.

Worrying him since his return from their honeymoon was his lack of occupation. He had made it clear to Sir

Alfred both before the marriage and since his return to Park Lane that he wished to do work of some sort.

It would be easy for his father-in-law to give him introductions either in the City or to some commerical enterprise where, even if he started in a small way, he would doubtless be able to make himself secure for the future.

Frank was anxious not to be entirely dependent on Edith for the rest of his life, and he felt too that if he did not have some reasonable excuse for being away from his wife he would be unable to stand the strain of unrelieved intimacy.

At the moment if he wanted to shop, to go for a walk, to do anything other than sit about the house, Edith wished to be with him.

Sooner or later he would give way to his natural inclinations and tell her that he could not stand it.

A little of her company in the morning and in the evening after a hard day's work he felt might be quite enjoyable, but for her to be beside him every hour of the day and night was unbearable.

Sir Alfred had been almost enthusiastic at the idea of finding Frank a job before they were married, but since they had come back to London he had been elusive on the subject.

He was working hard and seemed in some ways to be on edge. There were difficulties in the City; prices were falling, not abnormally, but Frank sensed that Sir Alfred was worried.

He talked with his old confidence but his words lacked the ring of conviction. He looked tired, too, and older.

Nonetheless Frank felt that he must insist on Sir Alfred taking his own position seriously. He asked Edith to remind her father, but at the mere hint of Frank having other interests beside herself she became sulky.

"I can't think why you want to work," she said. "We live here free and Daddy is going to pay two thousand pounds a quarter into the bank for us on a joint account, he told me so last night. That's eight thousand a year, Frank, you can't want more than that."

"It isn't only a question of money," Frank said patiently.

Then as an afterthought he added,

"Perhaps in a way it is. I'd like to have money of my own."

"It is your own now you are married to me," Edith answered.

But Frank knew that Edith was well aware of the power that her money gave her over her husband. Already once or twice in their quarrels she had referred to her income and to Frank's poverty.

He knew that to escape he must find work.

He could not understand Sir Alfred's hesitation. There were few stockbroking firms in the City who would not be delighted to take in the "gold-fingered" financier's son-in-law.

"I shall talk to him again tonight," Frank thought to himself as he finished breakfast. "I shall insist that he gives me an introduction to someone."

He rose to his feet. The newspaper was on the floor where he had flung it; as he saw it he sighed. He knew only too well how the morning must be spent—pacifying Edith.

He had an impulse to go out of the house without seeing her, but sooner or later he must return and a scene then would inevitably occur. It was best to get it over and done with.

He looked at the pictured smiling face of the little actress who had caused all the trouble; he had admired her originally because, with her fair hair and blue eyes, she had reminded him vaguely of Helga.

Suddenly Frank felt that he could bear this no longer. He saw himself getting old with Edith nagging at him day after day, eternally at his side, criticizing and commenting on every action of his, however harmless and commonplace.

Today was only one of many incidents. Because he had smiled and chatted with a waitress at a tea-shop there had been a scene which had lasted far into the night, Edith sobbing and reviling him.

She was making him self-conscious where any woman was concerned and he could think of nothing which would effectively cure her of her suspicions.

At first Frank told himself that it must be his fault, that Edith sensed that his heart was not hers and therefore felt herself denied a reciprocation of her own whole-hearted affection.

But as he grew to know his wife better he came to the conclusion that her temperamental storms came from some other, quite irrational, cause.

Frank tore up the newspaper he held in his hand and flung it into the waste-paper basket. It was better out of the way in case Edith, when she recovered, should see it again. He walked into the hall and went towards the stairs.

William's voice from the library door stopped him.

"If you please, sir," he said, "Sir Julian Holme wishes to speak to you on the telephone."

"To me?" Frank asked in surprise.

He knew Sir Julian very slightly. He was a great friend of Sir Alfred, but he had only been twice to the house when Frank was there.

"Yes, sir, Sir Julian asked particularly for you," William said.

"I wonder what on earth he wants? Frank thought, as he hurried into the library and picked up the telphone.

"Is that you, Swinton?" said Sir Julian's deep voice.

"Yes, sir," Frank answered.

"I wondered if you and your wife would care to dine with me next Wednesday. I have a small party of young people and I thought we might go on after dinner to a theatre."

"Thank you very much, we'd like to come," Frank answered.

There was a pause, then Sir Julian asked:

"How is your father-in-law?"

The question was asked casually enough, yet Frank, surprised at the whole conversation, was instinctively aware that this question was the real reason for Sir Julian's communication.

"Very well," Frank answered, "very well indeed, I think."

"Not worried at all? You don't think he's anxious?"

"Not that I know of," Frank said doubtfully. "As a matter of fact I haven't seen him this morning or last night. He went out to dinner and didn't return until after my wife and I had gone to bed. Yesterday morning he seemed as usual."

"Oh, yesterday morning!" Sir Julian said, as if that was no answer to his question. "Oh well, I only wondered. The market is in a precarious state, you know, Swinton, and Kalfridrs are falling."

"Seriously?" Frank asked.

"Enough to worry small fry like myself," Sir Julian replied, "but I expect your father-in-law will hardly notice the difference."

He gave a short laugh without much mirth about, then added abruptly:

"Wednesday, then, at seven-forty-five. Good-bye."

There was the click of a replaced receiver in Frank's ear; slowly he put down his earpiece.

The conversation made him think. He was certain that the reason for the telephone-call had been to enquire about Sir Alfred. But why hadn't Sir Julian telephoned the financier himself?

They were such old friends that surely it would have been quite a simple matter for him to ask point blank for the information he required.

Frank had naturally heard Sir Alfred speak of Kalfridrs.

It was a gold mine in which he had been keenly interested for the past two months; he believed in its prospects and he had urged a great many of his personal friends to invest heavily in the shares which had been soaring because of the satisfactory reports which had been received from West Africa.

Sir Alfred had been so confident and so certain of his information that the news that the shares were dropping could only mean that some entirely unforeseen hitch had occurred within the last few days.

Yet as he turned the matter over in his mind Frank remembered Sir Alfred's restlessness in the past weeks.

Could the nervous strain which he himself had sensed rather than noticed in his father-in-law be in any way due to this?

Sir Julian was a level-headed, cautious investor, he was not likely to get hysterical at the first hint of trouble or to bother about small losses. If we were worried it must mean that there was real anxiety.

Slowly Frank paced up and down the library floor, debating with himself whether he would telephone Sir Alfred in the City and tell him what had just occurred.

Then he decided that after all he had little or nothing to say.

He would tell his father-in-law of the conversation when he returned that evening, he could mention Sir Julian's questions casually and watch Sir Alfred's reception of them.

It was luncheon time before Edith was finally appeased, before she could be persuaded to bathe her swollen eyes and come down downstairs again for a meal.

She dressed quickly and carelessly so that when finally she appeared in the dining-room Frank noticed with a sense of irritation that short pieces of her hair had, as usual, escaped from the confines of a net, and that the velvet lapels of her coat needed brushing.

No maid, however conscientious, could keep Edith

111

tidy; her clothes seemed to magnetize dust even as the buttons seemed to fall from her gloves as soon as she tried to put them on.

There was always some little thing out of place, some small carelessness which spoiled the effect of anything she wore.

After a temperamental storm Edith did not look her best, her complexion was blotchy and her eyes half their usual size. Powder, badly applied, would seldom remain on her nose, but at least for the moment her tears had ceased.

She smiled tremulously across the table at Frank, and he noticed she managed to eat heartily of the various excellent dishes.

"What are your plans for this afternoon?" Frank asked.

"I've got a fitting at Lucille's for three o'clock," Edith replied.

"I'll drop you at Hanover Square and then take a good walk. I need some exercise."

"Oh, don't leave me," she protested. "Do come with me. You know how much I like you being there, and they are certain to do something terrible to my new clothes if you aren't there."

"I simply must get some exercise," Frank repeated.

"But we can walk afterwards," Edith argued, "we could send the car away and walk back."

Frank was well aware of Edith's idea of walking. Slowly, on high heels, she would wander past the shop windows, stopping every few yards; after twenty minutes or so she would exclaim that she was exhausted and insist on taking a taxi.

"I will take you in the Park after tea," he promised. "Keep the car and come back here as soon as you've finished, you'll be through by five o'clock, then if the evening is fine we will take a stroll."

"I wish you'd come with me," Edith pouted.

112

At the same time she realized by her husband's voice that he intended to have his own way."

Frank told her of Sir Julian Holme's invitation for Wednesday.

"How did your father seem this morning when you saw him?" he asked.

"Daddy? Oh, he was all right," Edith answered.

"You didn't think he was worried?"

"He was rather silent," she said, "and he didn't eat any breakfast, only drank his coffee and hurried off."

"Did he say what time he'll be back this evening?"

"I don't think so," Edith answered. "I can't remember if he's in to dinner or out. Shall I ring and ask?"

"No, it doesn't matter," Frank said.

But as he waited for Edith to get ready and as they drove towards Hanover Square in their smart black car he found his thoughts continually dwelling on Sir Alfred. Before they left the house he had again restrained an impulse to ring him up.

He felt that he wanted his father-in-law's quick, vital voice to reassure him, to tell him all was well, and only the fear of appearing ridiculous prevented him from obeying his instinct.

The afternoon was a change from the morning; a pale sun was striving to force its way through the grey clouds.

Frank stepped out briskly. He looked forward to his walk and to the two hours he would spend alone without his wife. At the corner of Bond Street and Brook Street he saw a newspaper boy. There was a poster in his hand. For a moment Frank stood still as he read:

GOLD MINE SENSATION
FINANCIAL CRISIS IN THE CITY

He ran across the road and thrusting sixpence into the boy's hand took a paper. For a moment he turned the pages wildly; in the Stop Press he found:

Following an authentic report received from West Africa at noon today there was a sensation in financial circles when it was learnt that the Kalfridr Gold Mine had closed down.

Frank hailed a taxi. For a moment he hesitated before giving the address—should he go straight to Sir Alfred in the City? He decided it would be best to go home and to telephone first.

As he was carried along, he wondered if he was being unduly perturbed; after all, Sir Alfred had never confided in him as regards his financial transactions.

He knew that his father-in-law was deeply interested in Kalfridrs and considered them one of the best speculations which had come on the market for years, but for all Frank knew he might easily have sold his shares in the last two or three days.

Yet if he had done so and saved his own money, he would be in the uncomfortable position of having boosted the merits of the mine to all his personal friends and made a fortune out of their loss.

Six Alfred's luck had been so phenomenal in the past that it was inconceivable to think that he could crash badly, yet Frank felt that in some way this unexpected crisis was serious.

Surely, if Sir Alfred had been in any way doubtful about the shares, he would, in the last twenty-four hours or so, have communicated with his best friend, Sir Julian Holme?

That he had not done so seemed to portend that he himself had been confident, in which case it was logical to suppose that he would be a very big loser.

When Frank arrived at Park Lane he paid off the taxi and ran up the steps. Before he could get out his key, however, the door was opened for him by William.

"Is there a message from Sir Alfred?" Frank asked.

"No, sir, but Mr. Winter is here," William answered. "I told him I didn't think you would be back until tea-time, but he insisted on waiting. He seems rather upset."

Frank put down his hat in the hall and walked into the library. He felt a foreboding of disaster.

Winter was Sir Alfred's confidential secretary at the office, he had been with the financier for over twenty-five years, and there was little that went on either in the City or in Sir Alfred's home of which he did not know.

It was Winter who paid the servants' wages, who saw to the insurances, who handled all Sir Alfred's private affairs as well as being continually at his side in the City office.

As he came into the library and heard William shut the door softly behind him, one look at Winter's face told Frank that his fears were not unfounded.

The man was standing in front of the fire turning his bowler hat round and round between nervous fingers.

"What is it?" Frank said abruptly.

Speaking hardly above a whisper, Winter answered: "Sir Alfred shot himself half an hour ago."

For a moment Frank could hardly take in the significance of what he heard. There was silence, and then in a voice broken by emotion, wavering and trembling on every syllable, Winter said:

"He couldn't face it, Mr. Swinton, he couldn't face it. He had bought Kalfridrs with every penny he possessed, he believed in them, and when he heard the news this morning he was like a man who had been dealt a mortal wound. He wouldn't go out to lunch, he wouldn't take any telephone-calls, he just sat there at his desk staring straight ahead of him.

" 'Leave me alone, Winter,' he said, 'tell them I want to be left alone.'

"I went in at half-past two and he was still sitting there. He didn't speak to me and I crept out again; a few minutes later we heard the shot."

"What is happening now?" Frank asked, with dry lips.

115

"They were getting the police when I left. I thought I'd better come here and tell you so that you could break it to Miss Edith."

Frank crossed the room and taking a cigarette out of a large silver box he lit it. Almost with surprise he noticed that his hand was trembling.

He could find no words to speak and could only stand trying to think, to realize the full horror of what Winter had just told him.

"In all the years I've known him," Winter went on, "Sir Alfred has never been one to put all his eggs in one basket. This time he seemed to go crazy. He believed in that mine, he had private information, he'd sent his own men out there, and he believed the stories they sent home to him.

"He must have been mad, Mr. Swinton. I've said to myself often: 'The Chief's taking a risk he's never taken before.' When he told me to mortgage the two houses I even argued with him."

"Mortgage the houses!" Frank ejaculated.

"He'd never done such a thing before," Winter said. "He mortgaged this house and all its contents and Wentworth Hall. He sold all his other shares, everything.

" 'This is the coup of my career, Winter,' he said to me. 'It will put me exactly where I want to be. After this you and I can retire.' "

Frank could see it all clearly, see the whole bitter story as Winter told it. If this mine has justified Sir Alfred's belief in it he would, indeed, have become a financial power.

He would have held the controlling interest of the mine itself and his fortune, already colossal, would have doubled and redoubled itself until his position in the City would have been beyond challenge.

There was a long silence. Frank saw that slow, agonizing tears were coursing their way down Winter's face. He had lost not only a Chief that he believed in, but a man that he loved.

Frank walked to the window.

"You better go back to the office, Winter," he said. "I'll wait here for my wife and break the news to her, then I will telephone you to find out what has happened. Will they bring him here, do you think?"

Winter blew his nose before he spoke.

"I don't know, Mr. Swinton," he answered, gulping back his tears and struggling for composure.

"In the meantime," Frank went on, "please don't say anything to the servants. Mrs. Swinton must be the first to know."

"Of course, sir, of course," Winter answered.

He walked towards the door, and as he reached it Frank turned towards him from the window and held out his hand.

"I'm sorry, Winter," he said; "I'm sorry for you too. I know you were fond of him."

Winter's emotion prevented him speaking and he hurried from the room.

Frank stood still, wondering what he should do. Should he telephone Edith at the shop or wait until she returned? He glanced at the clock on the mantelpiece. It was only just a quarter past three. Three-quarters of an hour ago Sir Alfred had been alive, and now . . .

Frank looked round him. So all this was mortgaged.

Quite suddenly he began to laugh. From his point of view the affair had its funny side. He had married money, money which had seemed secure, impregnable, and now it had been swept away from him almost before he had it in his grasp.

He knew quite well that Winter's story was not likely to be exaggerated; he was, perhaps, the only person in the world who had a true knowledge of Sir Alfred's dealings.

Frank saw himself back again where he had started, where every penny counted and there was a continual cry for money . . . Then he remembered this time he would not be alone . . . Edith would be with him, at his side.

He walked across the room to throw his half-smoked cigarette into the fire, and as he did so the front page of a newspaper caught his eye.

CANADA—THE LAND OF OPPORTUNITY

The words mixed themselves with the chaos of his thoughts. Suddenly they seemed to hold a personal significance for him. Canada—the land of opportunity!

He walked to the desk at which, four months ago, he had first seen Helga. He pulled open the top left-hand drawer and from a small box at the back he took a key.

Walking across the room he touched a spring in one of the panels, which flew back to reveal a safe. He opened it and stood staring at its contents.

Only Sir Alfred, Edith, and himself had access to this safe.

In it was kept Lady Steene's jewelry, which one day Edith would inherit, and a certain amount of cash which Sir Alfred liked to have handy in case money was required when the banks were closed.

Frank opened the cash-box and found that there was nearly ninety pounds in gold, besides some loose silver. He stood looking at it for some moments; finally he put out his hand and started to put it in his pockets.

In a tray underneath he found two twenty-pound notes. Only when the money was finally on his person did he ask himself what he meant to do.

He looked at the velvet boxes of jewellery on the tray above. They were Edith's. He had a rough idea that their value was between fifteen and twenty thousand pounds.

Sir Alfred had been a generous man to his invalid wife. Edith had also inherited from her mother an income of three hundred and fifty pounds a year.

On several occasions she had laughed about this to

Frank, saying it kept her in stockings if in nothing else.

With three hundred and fifty a year and the proceeds of the jewellery—Edith would not starve.

Frank closed the safe carefully and replaced the key; he sat down at the desk and wrote a short note to his wife. As he put it in an envelope and wrote her name on the outside, the clock struck half-past three.

He opened the door, and seeing no one in the hall, walked quickly upstairs.

In his own bedroom he collected together the links, expensive cigarette-cases, and various other articles of jewellery that Edith had given him during their engagement and married life.

When this was done he hesitated for a moment, then finding the passage outside empty he walked quickly up another flight of stairs to where the boxes were kept in an unfurnished room at the back of the house.

He came down again carrying a large bag which he packed swiftly, but before he had finished he heard a clock strike four.

Hastily he threw in a few more things, shut the bag, and taking down an overcoat from the wardrobe cautiously opened the door.

Looking down the well of the stairway he could see no one about. In the hall he put the note he had written to Edith in a prominent position on the card-table; then he let himself out of the front door.

He walked swiftly along the pavement until he saw a taxi. He hailed it.

"Euston Station," he said to the man, "and hurry."

CHAPTER EIGHT

1918

There was the rustle of a starched apron and the sweet smell of narcissi. Frank opened his eyes to see the nurse arranging a bowl of spring flowers on his bedside-table.

"Are those for me?" he said, with a smile.

"They are," she answered. "They came up from my home in the country this morning."

"You are a darling," Frank said.

She dimpled at him for a moment and then with mock severity added:

"Now, Captain Wode, how often have I told you not to flirt with the nurses on duty."

"If you want me to keep that rule," Frank answered, "you will have to get transferred to another ward."

He put out his hand to take hers but she eluded him, and with a little laugh moved away.

The spring sunshine came through the long windows, glinting on her dark chestnut curls which escaped from the severe white cap of starched muslin. She was a very pretty nurse—all the nurses were in Lady Hood's Hospital. She chose them carefully from among the daughters of her friends.

Frank had been lucky to be sent to number 349 Carlton House Terrace, when he had been wounded. It was a coveted hospital to be at and there was a selection committee who decided which officers should be admitted.

Most of the patients were men whose names had figured on the lists of society hostesses before the war.

That Frank had been admitted he knew was due to the fact that after his name he was now entitled to add the magical letters V.C.

He was pleased with the distinction—it gave him a glamour, and he was experiencing for the first time what hero worship could mean.

The nurses made a fuss of him and visitors to the ward generally made some excuse to come and speak to him before they left.

It was not in winning the V.C. that he had been wounded; the incident which had gained him the most coveted decoration in the British Army had taken place over a year ago, and he had not come to England until he had been severely wounded in the leg and in the head.

A stretcher case, he had been transferred from the Canadian Base Hospital to Lady Hood's Home in London.

By his bed was the temperature chart bearing his name, "Captain Wyndham Wode, V.C."

After seven years, Frank had become used to the sound of the new name with which he had christened himself on that memorable journey between London and Liverpool.

He had never been certain what made him choose anything so fanciful.

Ten years later it might have been useful as a label for a film star arriving in Hollywood, but it was certainly no advantage on the bitterly cold morning, with snow in the clouds and slush under foot, that he had first set foot on Canadian soil.

The men with whom he associated that first year when he was struggling to make a living had no use for fancy names.

121

They called him Bill or Bert or anything else which came easily to the tongue and quickly to their minds.

Frank's arms, even after three months' illness, had not entirely lost their strength, developed during that year of probation in a new country.

He had left England a man who had lived by his wits; he had learnt in Canada to be a man who lived by his muscles.

Strangely, he had never been so happy in his life. He found himself in lumber camps, in ranches, sharing bed and board with men who had sweated for their living all their days and who had learnt to be good fellows and the best possible companions because of it.

In England Frank had lived in a world of women; in Canada he learnt to know men, strong men who knew the true meaning of manhood and all that it should be without the decadence and vice of cities and civilization to ruin it.

Almost without realizing it Frank grew with them and became one of them. It was a wild life, nearly always precarious, and often dangerous.

He learnt to rely on himself in a way he would never have thought possible in the old days when he depended upon chance or charity to bring him the wherewithal to live and eat.

He had always counted on his personal charm and it stood him in good stead now, but where before it had been a snare for weak women, it now became the means to good fellowship with men.

The money with which he had arrived had been useful, but it was his charm that ensured him a helping hand in whatever circumstances he found himself.

Frank grew physically hard; his outlook broadened and he became mentally more worthy of his new muscle. With his capacity for living in the present he found it easy to forget England and all that he had left there.

He had always been one of those people who live

from day to day, and soon it had seemed to him almost unreal that such a person as Frank Swinton had ever existed, either struggling, or in the luxury of a Park Lane home, as the idle husband of a rich wife.

He loved Canada, it meant more to him than any other place he had been to in his life, yet when England entered the war against Germany there was some tie between himself and his own country, which convinced him that he must fight for her.

He joined up immediately and landed in France with the first Canadian Expeditionary Force in 1915. They were a magnificient body of men but Frank found himself bewildered, with his fellow Canadians, by the fact that they could not get to grips with the enemy.

They were all men of strong physique and it drove them nearly mad to sit day after day in water-logged trenches being riddled and wounded by shell-fire without a sight of the men who had fired on them and without chance of retaliation.

They kept their spirits up, often singing some of the songs they had learnt round the camp-fire.

In after years Frank, recalling his memories of the war, found more vivid than the mud and misery, the stench and the desolation, the picture of men's faces lit by bursting shells, their heads thrown back while from their throats came the melodious crooning sounds of the backwoods.

After six months in France, Frank got his commission. His men liked him, he was popular and had no trouble either with the rank and file or with his superior officers.

There was a cheerful, democratic unity among the Canadian forces which at times horrified the more staid and class-conscious British officers, but there was little friction and the discipline was good.

In the years he had been in Canada women had entered very little into his sphere of life.

123

There had, of course, been flirtations and many women had found him charming and wanted to bind him closer to them by the ties of affection.

After years of separation, however, he still judged them all in comparison with Helga.

Naturally, as time passed, the agony of separation from her grew less, he did not think about her or dream about her as often as he had; at the same time, whenever a woman came into his life he found himself comparing her looks and character with the girl he had loved so passionately.

He wondered what had happened to her, and when war came he was aware that another barrier had risen between them—they were fighting on opposite sides.

Had Helga sent a husband or lover to the front; did she sometimes think that perhaps a German bullet would mean the end of the man she had once loved?

But on the whole Frank was not given to sentimental musings, and if his love for Helga did alter his life and still determined his interest in other women he continued as he had always done to enjoy, if he could, the existing moment.

He won his V.C. in what the despatches called "a singularly gallant manner," but at the time, as when most deeds of valour are done, he had no idea that he was doing anything unusual.

An attack had been planned, and at zero hour Frank and his company went over the top and headed for the German trenches.

In a bewildering barrage of shots, shouted commands, and a general mêlée, the advance was almost stopped by a sudden storm which beat in the faces of the troops and soaked them to the skin in a few minutes. The rain was blinding in its intensity.

Frank and another man lost themselves; finally they came upon a half-derelict pill-box which they saw looming dimly through the mist on their left flank.

124

Inside was a scene of desolation. A shell had destroyed the roof and damaged the sides, and there were, it appeared, about a dozen men either dead or dying on the floor.

"My God! What a bloody mess!" Frank's companion murmured.

Frank stood in the half-broken doorway staring out, trying to see what had happened, and then in a sudden flash he saw coming towards them aline of grey figures.

"A counter attack!" he gasped, even as his friend realized what was happening.

Desperately they looked about them; there were the abandoned machine-guns, the dead men in a pool of blood beside them, one man with his head blown off, another in a crumpled heap.

Frank had no idea what he said or shouted to his friend; the next thing he knew was that they were both working at the guns.

Frank heard his own voice using strange words, he felt somehow a desire for revenge and laughed to see the men in front of him crumple even as those had who lay at his side.

The Germans immediately in front wavered; the guns fired on, there was the steady flashing flame, the automatic drilling of bullets; then—for a moment Frank could hardly believe it—the advancing soldiers turned.

While the Allies' attack had failed, so had the counter stroke of their enemies.

He turned to his friend, a cry of triumph on his lips, which was checked as he saw that the second gun was silent and that lying beside it was a still figure. The man was dead, shot between the eyes.

Frank got to his feet and as he did so a voice from the darkness on the other side of the pill-box said:

"That was well done."

"Who is it?" Frank asked.

He groped in his pocket for matches and picking his

way over the dead bodies that littered the floor crept to where, against an unbroken piece of wall, lay the man who had spoken.

"A damn' fine piece of work," the man said.

"Thank you," Frank answered.

The light of his match glimmered on the crown on the other's shoulder. "Are you wounded, sir?" he asked.

"They've got me in both legs," came the answer.

Half an hour later Frank carried into the front line Major Sir Henry Rankin.

He had made a gallant journey with the man, who was no light weight, on his back, but it was Sir Henry's description of Frank at the machine-guns which gained him the V.C., not the merciful action by which he saved a superior officer's life.

Both combined, however, to make him somewhat of a hero and as he was the first man in his division to receive the Victoria Cross he was fêted and complimented and, what was more important, promoted.

He began to believe, as did some of the men who served under him, that he bore a charmed life.

In that particular encounter nearly seventy-five per cent of the Canadian strength in that part of the line had been wounded.

New drafts came up to replace them, and again, after months of fighting, more and yet more men, but still Frank went on without even a scratch or anything more serious than badly blistered heels and a mild attack of influenza.

It began to be a joke among his companions that when there was some particularly dangerous job to be done Frank was sent to do it, because the Colonel was quite certain that he would turn up again safe and sound.

The men even became superstitious about him and preferred him to lead them into the front line rather than any of the officers in whom they had less confidence.

But at last a shell burst almost on top of Frank one day when he was making a round of his posts and he knew nothing more until he found himself in the base hospital and was told that he had already been there for nearly three weeks.

When he had finally come to England and had been inspected by the surgeons at Lady Hood's hospital they told him quite frankly that his war service was over.

His left leg was injured from hip to ankle and although the leg itself could be saved and not amputated, he would have to walk with crutches for some months and it was doubtful if ever again he would manage without a stick.

The wound in his head was not serious, but he would have scars on his forehead and cheek from shell splinters which by some miracle of luck had just missed his left eye.

Frank's splendid constitution stood him in good stead now.

He began to recover his health in an amazing way and was out of bed and beginning to limp about far quicker than the doctors expected; nevertheless, they bade him go slow and he was content to do as he was told.

He was happy at Lady Hood's and fully aware how fortunate he was in being admitted as a patient.

Today, the first morning of spring when the chill of the February air was belied by the gaiety of the sunshine, Frank found himself thinking of the future and wondering what he could make of his life.

He faced the fact quite sanely that he would in many ways be crippled.

The jobs he had done in Canada would no longer be open to him. A decision did not have to be made quickly, but sooner or later, he knew, he must face the issue.

His thoughts were interrupted by a V.A.D. coming down the ward towards him.

She was a particular favourite of his, a very pretty girl, who, had war not been in progress, would have been dancing night after night at fashionable balls and leading the glamorous life of a rich and beautiful débutante.

As it was she spent her days scrubbing floors, obeying commands of better-trained women, and doing her little bit to cheer up the men who had been fighting for their country.

She was slim and graceful, and not even the starched cotton dresses and stiff aprons could hide the beauty of her figure.

She came towards Frank's bed and he smiled at her; then he noticed that someone else, a small woman dressed in grey, was following her.

For a moment he did not recognize her, then in horror he saw it was his wife, Edith!

"Here is a visitor for you, Captain Wode," the V.A.D. said brightly. "Won't you sit down?" she added to Edith, pulling a comfortable armchair near to Frank's side.

"Thank you," Edith said in a low voice.

Frank knew at once that she was nervous. She had not altered much, he thought grimly. The grey of her coat was a particularly unbecoming colour and under her velvet toque wisps of dark hair escaped down her neck.

Her complexion was more sallow than he remembered it and her hands, encased in grey kid gloves, fidgeted with a bag of which the handle was broken.

At the same time she looked prosperous, her fur collar was of real fox, there was a glint of diamonds at her neck, while the pearl ear-rings, if they were not genuine, were certainly an expensive imitation.

The minute that it took for Edith to be seated in the armchair and for the nurse to leave them gave Frank time to regain his composure. He thought quickly of what he was to say and do.

He remembered that his head was bound in bandages, there were strips of plaster over his left cheek, and that since he had last seen Edith he had shaved his moustache. He was now clean-shaven.

Before he spoke Edith opened her bag and taking out a photograph torn from a newspaper held it towards him.

"I came to see you," she said, "because of this."

Frank, still without speaking, took it from her and saw that it was a photograph taken from the *Tatler* of two or three weeks before.

It showed him in a group of officers with the caption, *Celebrities at Lady Hood's Hospital in Carlton House Terrace.* Their names were inscribed underneath—his as *Captain Wyndham Wode, the gallant Canadian V.C.*

Frank did not hurry over his inspection of the photograph while he wondered what attitude to take. It was so like Edith, he thought, to do something unexpected and in as awkward a manner as possible.

As he did not speak, Edith became visibly more nervous.

"You see, I thought I recognized the photograph," she said.

"Of me?" Frank asked.

He purposely made his voice low and languid, hoping that it would not be obviously reminiscent to his wife.

At last he understood the situation. She had come expecting to recognize him immediately and now she was not certain of him.

"I thought," Edith said hesitatingly, "I thought you were my husband."

Had her voice in any way shown signs of emotion or had there been a suspicion of tears in her eyes Frank might have relented and revealed himself.

But there was the same hard yet whining tone in her voice which he had never forgotten. Edith with a grievance . . . Edith thinking she had been affronted and badly treated.

How well he knew it, and how well, seeing her again, he remembered the exhausting and degrading scenes which generally followed her unfounded accusations and suspicions.

Frank simulated surprise.

"Your husband!" he said. "You thought I was your husband!"

"Yes. You see, I lost my husband some years ago," Edith answered dropping her eyes. "Not by death; he just disappeared, and your photograph was so extraordinarily like him—except he had a moustache and was much thinner—but now . . ."

She hesitated.

"Now you see me you are disappointed," Frank interposed.

"Well . . . I mean . . . I don't know," Edith said, incoherent and as ever hopeless at expressing herself. "In a way I want to see my husband again, and in a way I don't, if you know what I mean. I hated him for making me so miserable."

"You shouldn't do that, you know," Frank said gravely. "Very few people are worth hating."

"Oh, I don't know," Edith answered quickly. "I am quite happy without him really, at the same time I'd like to see him or to have the opportunity of hearing what became of him."

'An opportunity you'll never have, pray God!' Frank thought; aloud he said:

"Do you live in London?"

Edith nodded.

"Yes, I've a little house in Regent's Park. I share it with a cousin of mine. We are very comfortable. She was let down by a man, too."

"Really?" Frank said.

"Yes, he promised to marry her, but when he got out to India with his regiment he wrote and broke it off. She was awfully upset for a long time and then she decided that she would do without men in her life, and as I thought the same, we decided to keep house together."

She paused.

"At the same time it is tiresome not knowing if one's husband is alive or dead."

"It must be," Frank agreed. "But if you haven't heard from him for some years I should think there is every chance of his being dead by now."

"This terrible war!" Edith said.

Although she said the words Frank had an idea that they meant very little to her. She seemed to have grown neither older nor less self-centered than when he last saw her.

He could imagine her living with another woman in compact and genteel comfort, doing nothing for anyone, leading a dull, selfish life with an almost unpleasant contentment.

"Were you fond of your husband?" he asked.

He knew it was hardly the question he should put to a wife he had brutally deserted, at the same time there was a humour in the situation that he could not resist.

"I adored him," Edith said seriously, "and of course when we married he adored me too. The sudden shock of my father's death must have entirely deranged his mind; we ... I mean I ... think the real explanation of his disappearance is that he must have lost his memory."

Frank could hardly resist laughing. This was so like Edith's vanity not to face the truth that he had married her for her money and abandoned her when she had none.

Instead, her first rage and fury over, she was prepared to pretend even to herself that there was some very strange motive for her husband's disappearance.

"Didn't you search for your husband when he disappeared?" Frank asked.

He had often wondered if Edith had told the police about him.

She shook her head.

"It was hardly a matter for me to discuss with outsiders," she said primly.

Again Frank realized that her vanity had brought a pride to her aid which at least had been useful to him.

She picked up the photograph and put it back in her bag; pulling on one of her gloves which she had taken off she rose to her feet.

"I am sorry to have bothered you, Captain Wode," she said, "but there was just a chance that you might have been my husband, and I felt it my duty to make sure."

"I am sorry you have had your journey here for nothing," Frank said politely.

"Oh, that's quite all right," Edith answered. "My cousin is waiting outside for me in our little car. She drives us herself since our chauffeur had to go to the war."

"That's very nice for you," Frank said.

Quite seriously Edith answered:

"Yes, isn't it?"

She said good-bye, turned, and left him.

"Completely unaltered," Frank thought as he watched her disappearing through the door at the end of the ward.

Always Edith would find someone to look after her, to do things for her, not because she was attractive or charming or because she inspired affection, but because she was so helpless and hopeless.

Like a piece of ivy she had to be supported by something stronger than herself, and once she had fastened herself on to someone they would have to take desperate measures, as he had, to get free.

He wondered about the cousin and felt rather sorry for her; he hoped that she was a masterful, strong-minded woman who would keep Edith in her place and deal firmly with her when she became temperamental.

Frank realized from what he had escaped and he lay

back on his pillows with closed eyes feeling for a moment quite weak.

Supposing he had been unable to bluff Edith, supposing she had insisted that she recognized him?

He thought with horror of going back to her, taking up their life together again, subjecting himself to the petty scenes, suspicions, and the hopeless incompatability of their minds.

Looking back at the past he remembered Edith's indifference to theatres, to books, to the newspapers, to all the events taking place in the world around her.

He suspected now that she was far more concerned with food coupons than with the casualty lists, with the restrictions of petrol than with the winning or losing of the war.

She was not to blame, she was just incapable of concentrating on anything which did not touch her personally.

"It was a surprise for you to have a visitor," said a voice.

Frank opened his eyes to see the pretty V.A.D. beside him, a tea-tray in her hand.

"And after all she hadn't come to see me," Frank said.

"How terribly disappointing for you."

"Yes, wasn't it?" Frank answered lightly. "She thought I was somebody else whom she had once known in the dim, distant past."

"I expect it was all a hoax to get your autograph," the V.A.D. said smiling at him. "I must say she didn't look like it, but I can't tell you some of the people we get here after celebrities like yourself."

"If you tease me any more," Frank threatened, "I shall get up and kiss you."

"You'll do nothing of the sort," she said quickly, "I shall get the sack, and you'll be transferred to another hospital and not half such a nice one, I assure you."

"Well, you wait and see when I get my new crutches tomorrow," Frank promised.

Laughing at him over her shoulder the V.A.D. hurried away to serve tea to the other occupants of the ward.

The new crutches took a little bit of manipulating at first. They gripped him above the elbow instead of hoisting him in the old-fashioned way under the arms.

After some rather unsteady trial trips round the garden, Frank got used to them and shortly attained the privileges of more convalescent officers and was allowed out of hospital during the day.

He, like the others, enjoyed luncheon at the Piccadilly and a matinée afterwards, finding that wartime London, even after four years of war, was doing its best to keep the men in khaki and in blue cheerful and happy.

At Lady Hood's Hospital the sick men wore their uniforms, but were supplied with a blue armband which barred them from obtaining a drink anywhere.

Needless to say the armbands were easily detachable and before entering a restaurant or a bar were quickly placed in the pockets of their tunics.

About the middle of March, Frank was sitting in a small bar off Shaftesbury Avenue which he very often frequented on his days out when he had nowhere better to go, when a man entered whom he had not seen for nearly ten years.

Without thinking, Frank smiled in recognition and instantly the man crossed to where he was sitting.

"Good heavens, Swinton," he said, "I didn't recognize you for the moment. Where the devil have you been all these years?"

Only when he addressed him by name did Frank realize that he had made a mistake and revealed his identity, but feeling it was too late to draw back now, he held out his hand in greeting.

"I might ask you the same thing, Herman," he answered.

The man sat down beside him.

"My name's Herbert Moore now, old man," he said in a low voice. "Of course the whole thing is ridiculous and as you know my people had lived in England for years before I was born, but Herman Müller is not a very popular combination these days."

Frank laughed. As it happened he had forgotten the man's surname.

"Herbert Moore it shall be," he said heartily, "and since we are exchanging confidences you might forget the Swinton. My name is Wyndham Wode."

Herbert Moore held out his hand solemnly.

"It's a bargain," he said.

"Well, tell me about yourself," Frank asked. "What are you doing?"

"You wonder why I am not in uniform," Herbert said quickly. "My age is all right—about the only thing that is. I've got a heart that wouldn't pass a test for canaries and every other form of organic complaint that any medical board has ever heard of."

"Bad luck!" Frank murmured sympathetically.

"So I'm in the War Office," Moore said ruefully, "not with the red-tabs, of course, but in the casualty-list department and a very depressing job it is. I have just come from there, this is my afternoon off, and I have come to cheer myself up with a drink."

"Have one with me," Frank said, signalling to the barman.

"I see you are in the Canadians," Moore said. looking at the badge on Frank's shoulder. "Got a whole lot of the casualties come in this morning. Do you know a Major Paul Knowles? . . . He's dead."

"Not Tubby Knowles!" Frank said. "My God, has he gone too? He was a great friend of mine, one of the nicest fellows you could possibly imagine. I believe his

135

mother lives over here. I must go and see her. Tubby used to talk about her a lot; she is English, although his father was Canadian.

"She's got a big estate somewhere in the Midlands, I believe. He used to make all sorts of plans of how he'd live there after the war; we even talked about chicken-farming together!"

"Well, you'd better go and see the old lady," Moore said. "She might fix you up in the chicken farm if her son's gone. She sounds rich."

"I don't know her address," Frank answered.

"I can find that out for you."

"Can you? Well, it would be damn' good of you if you would, although I don't expect I shall get a chance of leaving London for some time."

"If you wrote to her she'd very likely come and see you."

"Well, if you give me her address I might think about it," Frank said, "I was fond of old Tubby."

They both had another drink and Herbert Moore suggested that Frank should come and see his flat, which was not far away in one of the quieter turnings off Regent Street.

Frank, who had nothing to do, was only too glad to agree, and he found Moore's flat, which was over a warehouse, small and cosy, but furnished in somewhat exotic taste.

"It isn't really a residential part," Moore explained, "but it's convenient for me and absolutely quiet. If the warehouse is opened twice a week, I'm unlucky—it's a storehouse for a big firm in Regent Street."

He got a bottle of whisky out of the cupboard and put it on the table with a siphon of soda.

"Help yourself," he said.

Frank poured himself out a drink.

"Happy days," he said.

Herbert sipped from his glass nervously; with a slightly hesitating manner he said, after a moment:

"I'd like to have a talk with you seriously, if you don't mind."

"Go ahead," Frank replied genially, feeling mellow and comfortable by the fireside, his crutches on the floor by his chair, his bad leg stretched out in front of him.

"Have you got any more money than you used to have?" Moore asked.

"No, and no prospects," Frank answered.

"Would you like to make some?" was the question.

"Frank laughed.

"Don't be silly," he said. "Have you ever known me not want to make money, or anyone who didn't for that matter? My dear Herbert, I assure you that when I come out of hospital I shall have mighty little cash; only a small but inadequate pension from my grateful country."

"Well, then, look here," Herbert said, leaning forward and lowering his voice, although there wasn't the slightest possibility of them being overheard. "I've got an idea that I've been wanting to put into operation for some time . . ."

* * *

"Did he talk about his home?"

"A great deal," Frank answered.

"And his dogs, Sam and Rover?"

"He was always wishing they were with him," Frank replied. "Once a hare came running up the line, straight across No Man's Land. The men were too surprised for the moment even to shoot at it and your son turned to me and said:

'I wish old Sam was here, he'd go mad with excitement!' "

"That's so like Gerald," his mother said. "His sport and his animals meant everything to him."

"We were both keen on the country, you see," Frank

explained. "We used to have long talks about the countryside.

"Of course I've spent a great many years of my life in Canada and he was interested in that, but he used to tell me about his home and the estate and how you were keeping it up, and we made all sorts of plans for the future. It seems strange they will come to nothing now."

"What sort of plans?"

"Oh, plans of what we were going to do. We had some wild idea that we might start a chicken farm together when the war was over.

"Gerald seemed to think it might pay if it was run on modern, up-to-date lines, and I have seen a bit of progressive management in that way abroad, so we were going to put out heads together and see what luck we had."

"You were going into partnership, you mean?"

"Well, if you like to put it like that. That's what Gerald used to say—'You and I together, Wyndham, we'll beat all the experts.'"

"He was always so enthusiastic," his mother said in a gentle voice.

"I'm afraid it wasn't what I'd call a partnership," Frank went on. "You see I'd not got any capital, but Gerald said he'd supply that all right. I was to be the manager, handle the sales and the business side. We reckoned that if we started with five hundred pounds we ought to see a profit in two years—at least Gerald was confident we should."

"Gerald was always confident," his mother whispered almost to herself, "he was confident he would come back."

"That's true," Frank said. "He never for one moment imagined that he was going to die, he was absolutely certain that he'd see the war out, be in at the finish, and after that ready for what the future might bring."

"And did you also plan where this farm was to be?"

"Oh, near you, of course," Frank answered. "That

138

was a foregone conclusion, Mrs. Marlow. I don't think Gerald ever wanted to do anything in which you didn't take an interest."

"Oh, Captain Wode, you make me so happy when you tell me that," Mrs. Marlow said, with tears in her eyes. "You see, my life was wrapped up in Gerald. His father died when he was very small and we were such friends; we meant so much to each other. When he went to school for the first time he said:

'It isn't that I mind going to school, Mummy, it's leaving you that makes me so unhappy.' "

Her voice broke.

"That's why it seems unbelievable that I shall never see him again. He was everything I had in the world, everything."

There was a long silence while Mrs. Marlow dried her tears and pulled her black felt hat a little lower so as to shade her face.

"It has made me very happy seeing you, Captain Wode," she said, when she could control her voice; "it was very kind of you to write to me. I had a wonderful letter from Gerald's Commanding Officer, but somehow it is not the same as meeting one of his friends and hearing about the little things he said, his actions day by day. I shall have a lot to think about now."

"I am so glad," Frank said.

"And there is one thing I want to say to you and you mustn't be angry with me or offended. This chicken farm that you and Gerald planned together . . . will you let me give you the capital to start it on your own?

"No, no," she said quickly as Frank made a vague gesture of protest, "I don't want you to think of it as a present from me, a woman, think of it as a present from Gerald. He would have wished it, you know yourself he would, and after all you can look at it this way—my money isn't very much use to me now that he's gone, I haven't got anything to spend it on."

"It's very kind of you indeed," Frank said.

"It is a very small return for what you have done for me, and I'd like it to be a memento of your friendship with my son," Mrs. Marlow said.

She got to her feet slowly, her hands still shaking slightly from the emotion through which she had passed and her face very pale.

"I will post you a cheque tonight," she said. "Goodbye, Captain Wode, and thank you from the very bottom of my heart."

Without saying more she let herself out of the door. Frank sat still, staring at the floor, his face quite expressionless. It was nearly a quarter of an hour later before a slam of the front door told him that Herbert Moore had returned. He came into the sitting-room immediately.

"Well?" he asked.

"For God's sake give me a drink!" Frank answered.

Herbert went to the cupboard, produced the whisky and put it at Frank's side. He waited until he had helped himself and drunk nearly half the glass before he asked again:

"Well?"

"I hated it," Frank said angrily, "it was a filthy job. It's a filthy idea."

"But a successful one?" Herbert questioned.

"She's posting a cheque for five hundred pounds tonight," Frank answered.

"My boy, you're a genius."

"I'm a swine, and you know it."

"Now we've been through this before," Herbert said soothingly. "You know quite well that it makes them happy. You know women—they want to hear little details, little scraps of conversation about their sons, the more commonplace the better.

"They all run true to form. You give them a certain amount of happiness and they give you a fat cheque. Who the hell is hurt by it? Certainly not the boy who is dead, he's beyond the reach of money at any rate."

"They're so damned eager to believe me. If it was more difficult to get it out of them, I wouldn't care so much."

"Oh, you're soft," Herbert Moore said. "Have another drink and forget it."

He well knew this mood of Frank's. Even when he had the details worked out of what seemed a foolproof plan he had had difficulty in persuading Frank to play the part allotted to him.

He was surprised, because in the old days Frank Swinton would have been the first person to jump at an opportunity of making easy money. The older man was more difficult to handle, but as he said bluntly—sentiment was an expensive luxury that a penniless man could ill afford.

In his position at the War Office Herbert could find out many details about the relations of casualties. He chose with great care the mothers of only sons, and made inquiries as to their financial position.

Only when everything was known about them did he persuade Frank to write a letter of condolence adding that he had known the dead officer in France, had served with him, and would like, if there was any chance of his mother being in London, to have a talk with her.

No unhappy, bereaved mother could resist such a letter and the mere fact that Frank was Captain Wode, the Canadian V.C., made them answer quickly and come to London at the first opportunity.

Frank could hardly bear his part; he could not become hardened to the tears the women shed, and as he said to Herbert, it was worse because it was so easy.

They told him about their sons, gave him all the answers to their questions, and were so grateful for the most commonplace and ridiculous bits of information.

Frank had now had five interviews and the result of each had been a cheque for five hundred pounds. Herbert had decided on this figure because it was not too large for these women of big incomes to find without consulting their lawyers or relations.

Whatever happened there must be no enquiries. Although it would be impossible to prove that Frank did not intend to start a chicken farm with some young man who was lying dead in France, at the same time legal advisers might make things very uncomfortable.

The flat was an ideal meeting-place, for there were no porters; it was easy to give someone an appointment at three o'clock and for Frank to arrive at a quarter of an hour before, and be there to let them in.

Only when they had gone and he had been thanked once again and promised a cheque in the morning did he invariably feel degraded, and a loathing of Herbert and all his ideas would sweep over him.

Herbert was clever enough to let him talk himself out, to take no notice of his insults, and was prepared not to press him too hard to arrange another interview until the last had faded a little from his mind.

Frank just kept trying to remember that he made the mothers happy. Money did not matter to them—why should he feel so ashamed of taking the cheques they almost begged him to accept?

But he hated it all, and every time he went to Herbert's flat he swore to himself it would be the last.

He had over a thousand pounds now placed to his credit at the bank.

That at least would give him a start when he was discharged; but when he suggested that they had enough Herbert begged him to try just one more, and cursing himself for his weakness, gave in.

He was getting much better every day, the electrical treatment was improving his leg and hip so that he could move without pain and much quicker. The spring had come and Easter was past, news from the Front was bad.

The Germans' big advance in March had dashed optimistic hopes of a finish before Christmas and there

142

were rumours of another offensive in which, if the Germans were successful, they planned to reach Paris.

Frank, leaving the hospital after luncheon, took a taxi to Herbert's flat. He had made an appointment to see Lady Stanbury at half-past two and he was afraid that he might be late.

However, it had not yet struck the half-hour when he arrived and propping the street door ajar so that Lady Stanbury could enter he got himself with difficulty up the steep flight of stairs that led to Herbert's flat.

When Lady Stanbury arrived he was standing waiting for her at the top and showed her into the sitting-room, suggesting with a smile that she take a seat near the fire.

"This is a nice little flat," she said approvingly. "Is it yours, Captain Wode?"

"No, it belongs to a friend of mine," Frank answered. "He lets me come here most afternoons to read or write my letters. One gets sick of the hospital after nearly six months of it, you know."

"I am sure you do," she answered.

Frank looked at her with interest. She was unlike the usual type of mother he interviewed. She was a tall woman and held herself erect with a splendid carriage; her clothes were not fashionable, but they were definitely expensive and well chosen.

"Here is someone with personality," Frank thought, "and someone of position."

And for the first time in all his interviews he felt afraid that Herbert had made a mistake.

"You wrote to me about Ronald," Lady Stanbury said clearly.

Her voice was neither weak nor tearful. Frank had an impression that here was a woman who was not hard but perfectly controlled.

Because she did not arrive with her handkerchief clutched in her hand ready to weep at the first mention of her son he was quite certain that she did not love him

143

less or miss him not as much as more hysterical mothers.

Frank had a sudden impulse to say:

"No, I did not know your son. I have made a mistake. Please go away."

Then pride and a certain fear of the consequences made him reply almost automatically:

"I happened to know your son very well in France. I thought perhaps you might like to see me."

"Please tell me about Ronald," Lady Stanbury said simply.

It was a more difficult interview than Frank had ever undertaken before. Lady Stanbury did not chatter, she did not ask many questions, she waited simply and with dignity for what Frank had to tell her.

Luckily Herbert had already supplied him with a list of the boy's accomplishments before the war started, and during the ensuing hour Frank made no mistakes.

Ronald Stanbury had had a great number of friends and his mother did not think it at all unusual that she had not known of his friendship with Frank.

Frank told her that they had met at the base on several occasions and left further details to Lady Stanbury's imagination, but when it came to the point when Frank usually spoke of the projected chicken farm he realized it would be a false note and entirely out of keeping with Ronald's character.

Herbert had made a mistake this time. Ronald Stanbury was a young man who enjoyed every form of sport and who rushed about from one place to the other in search of amusement.

It was unlikely that he would plan to settle down to the humdrum existence of a farm.

He gathered that Lady Stanbury was not only rich but that her son would have inherited a very large estate. The boy would not have specialized in chickens when there was a place of such a size to be managed and developed.

Frank, therefore, made no mention of the future, he merely talked of young Stanbury.

When he felt that he could say no more and it was dangerous to trade on his imagination he let a silence come into the conversation which should have preluded Lady Stanbury's departure.

To his surprise, however, instead of rising she said:

"Thank you, Captain Wode. I am very grateful to you indeed for all you have told me about Ronald. There is no need to tell you how much I value any information about him. But now talk to me about yourself. What are your plans for the future?"

CHAPTER NINE

Crosstrees Priory looked out over the green meadowlands which went down to the river Avon.

In the distance Bredon Hill, surmounted by its square tower, was silhouetted against the sky, and already on the fruit trees the budding blossom gave promise of a white and pink beauty in a few weeks' time.

Frank, standing on the terrace at the Priory, gazed over the countryside and found himself spell-bound by the beauty that was around him.

There was such a different atmosphere at Crosstrees Priory to that at Wentworth Hall, the only large country house that Frank had previously visited.

Here was no sign of pretentiousness, and while Lady Stanbury's guests were comfortable, there was, about all the arrangements made for them, an ease and intimacy which made them feel more members of the family than guests.

The house was large, far larger than Wentworth Hall, but with its low ceilings and lead-paned windows, its twisting oak staircases and small, cosy bedrooms, it was never awe-inspiring, but seemed in itself to give a welcome to everyone who stayed there.

Frank was surprised at first when Lady Stanbury asked him to go down for the weekend. He had, in fact, hesistated a little, nervous as to whether to accept or not.

"If you are wondering whether it would be possible from a hospital point of view," Lady Stanbury said, not understanding the motive for his hesitation, "don't worry. I know Lady Hood very well, in fact she is one of my oldest friends; I will speak to her and I know she will allow you to come.

She smiled.

"It will be no exertion; we will motor down and you can be back in London on Monday in time for treatment."

Frank did not need to let himself be persuaded. He had taken a liking to Lady Stanbury.

Although he was slightly afraid of her, feeling that here was someone whom it would be hard to deceive, he was deeply interested in someone who was entirely different from any woman he had ever met before.

As he grew to know her better he realized that her grief was very real and that by the death of her only son she had lost all that she most cared for in the world.

In her home it was obvious that the servants and tenants adored her; they looked on her not only as their employer but also as a friend, they came to her for advice and acted upon it.

Quite the most interesting member of the house party, yet it was not obvious why one should think so, was Colonel Harrison, Lady Stanbury's cousin.

He was a quiet, well-made man of about forty-six, whose appearance was rather nondescript.

Yet from the first moment that Frank shook hands with him he was conscious that here was somebody of distinction.

Colonel Harrison very rarely aired his opinions; when he did speak his conversation was of interest and seemed to be given with an air of authority.

The rest of the party listened to him with attention and Frank had the impression that they, too, accorded

Colonel Harrison a respect out of proportion to his appearance and rank.

The house party did little. They sat on the terrace in the sunshine, read, talked, the more energetic ones played tennis, and they all went to bed early; yet Frank told himself that never before in his life had he enjoyed anything so much.

By Sunday he was depressed to think that tomorrow his good time would be over and that he must return to London and the hospital.

Everyone had been very kind to him and particularly Lady Stanbury herself, who seemed to go out of her way to show him her home and the countryside and to interest him in the people who were staying with her.

"I have always wanted money," Frank thought to himself in his bedroom.

He lay in the curved four-poster bed, black with age, and looked out through the diamond-paned windows on to the garden below.

"But," he went on, "this sort of thing can't be bought; other people, however rich, couldn't live in this house, couldn't be part of it in the same way."

On Sunday evening Frank, sitting in the garden, was joined by Lady Stanbury.

"It is peaceful here, isn't it?" she said.

"I can't tell you how much I have enjoyed every moment of my visit," Frank said impulsively.

There was no doubt about the sincerity in his voice. Lady Stanbury smiled and for a moment her hand rested on his arm.

"I am so glad," she said. "I wanted you to see Ronnie's home."

There was a moment's silence, then as if she put the thought of her son firmly behind her she said briskly:

"Captain Wode, I asked you down here for another reason. I gathered from your conversation that you were not sure of your future and that you had no special plans for when you are discharged from the Army.

148

"The fact that you were Ronnie's friend, and also your own brilliant war record made me think that it would be a pity that someone like yourself should not, at any rate until the end of the war, go on helping us to win.

"So quite deliberately, although I wanted you to enjoy yourself as well, I asked you here to meet my cousin, Colonel Harrison."

Frank did not speak or interrupt, but she saw that she had his attention and went on:

"I am going to be quite frank with you, Captain Wode, and it is with my cousin's consent that I speak. I don't think—in fact I am sure that you have no idea who he is; very few people do know except those who work with him and who come under his authority.

"He is in the senior branch of the British Intelligence. He holds Army rank, but as I think you very likely know, there are several branches of the intelligence service, Naval and Military.

"But apart from all this there is the most important and the most secret branch of all and in this my cousin is in a position of great authority.

"There are others, of course, besides him, but that need concern neither of us; quite frankly, you know now as much as I know myself. David Harrison is a 'mystery man', but one for whom I have the greatest affection and respect."

"I somehow felt there was something unusual about him," Frank said.

"And you were right," Lady Stanbury went on. "Now, Captain Wode, you will have an idea as to why I wanted you to meet him. I had already spoken to him about you before you met. I wanted, as I have already said, to do something for one of Ronnie's friends, and I wanted also to do something, however small, for the country for which he died.

"David Harrison will come and talk to you himself, but I felt that you would rather I explained first who he was and why on such a short acquaintance he should approach you."

Frank tried to murmur his gratitude, but Lady Stanbury brushed his words to one side.

"You can only thank me," she said, "by coming here whenever you feel like it and making it a home. You know I shall always be glad to see you."

This was something that Frank had never anticipated, and after he had had a talk with Colonel Harrison he was even more surprised at the turn of events.

He was told that there was work he could do and that if he cared to offer his services in that capacity his discharge could be speeded up and as soon as he was well enough to leave the hospital Colonel Harrison would have need of him.

He was excited at the whole idea even while he was apprehensive of his own capabilities. Colonel Harrison smiled when he spoke modestly of his ability to be useful.

"It isn't only brains we require, Wode," he said, "it's the right type of men, and they are difficult enough to get hold of these days. I will be frank with you and say that the fact that you have come from Canada may be a distinct advantage.

"It would be more difficult for people to check up on who you were and what your movements are likely to be. Half the trouble, I don't mind telling you, in our profession is the fact that men have homes and friends."

It was after this interview that Frank thought guiltily of Herbert Moore. He knew that the first thing he must do was to drop such a discreditable association.

Colonel Harrison had obviously taken him at his face value and on Lady Stanbury's recommendation as Ronnie's friend, but in the future his movements would have to be particularly circumspect and Herbert Moore was an undesirable acquaintance who was best forgotten.

He thought of writing and then decided that that

would be a mistake—the old adage of never committing anything to paper came to his mind.

The telephone at the hospital was also likely to be overheard, but here at Crosstrees Priory he felt it would be easier to speak with complete safety from the small morning-room where there was a telephone.

When the rest of the house party had gone up to dress for dinner he asked the butler to switch the line through, and having seen that the door was firmly closed he picked up the receiver and asked for Herbert Moore's number.

After a moment or two he heard himself connected and Moore's voice answering:

"Hello, who is it?"

"Hello," Frank said, "it's Wode speaking. I'm on a long-distance line, can you hear me?"

"Perfectly," came the reply.

"Good," Frank said. "Now listen to me, Herbert. This little business that you and I have discussed and been interested in lately has got to finish.

"I can't explain why over the telephone but I can assure you that I have every reason for saying this. Also for the present I think it better that we don't meet. You understand?"

There was a pause and then Herbert Moore said deliberately:

"No, I don't understand."

"I have made it quite clear," Frank said.

"You have made it clear what you want," Herbert answered, "but I am afraid I can't accept your proposition, Swinton."

It was obvious from the tone of his voice and from the use of Frank's real name that Herbert was going to be nasty.

"I'd better try to pacify him," Frank thought.

"No, look here, old man," he said. "This is of great importance to me."

"And to me also."

"Yes, I know," Frank went on, "and we have been very lucky, but I can't promise you that in the present circumstances there is any question of that luck continuing."

"I think that's for me to say," Moore answered. "I already have some very interesting particulars for you."

"Well, you can put them in the fire," Frank said angrily.

"Oh, I don't think so, and I think you will find that is a very unwise attitude for you to take up," Moore said. "I want to see you. Will you please come here to the flat at three-thirty on Tuesday without fail.

"I can't manage it," Frank answered.

"Oh, yes, you can," Moore went on, "and if you don't I shall come to the hospital and see you."

"My God!" Frank ejaculated, and feeling it was unwise and pointless to say any more he put down the receiver.

What was he to do? he wondered. Moore was going to turn nasty; he obviously had every intention of going on with the scheme which was proving very lucrative and no trouble to him.

Frank had never liked the man and had known perfectly well that in the past he was notoriously "a sharp customer."

He cursed himself for getting mixed up with him in the first place, at the same time he realized that if it had not been for him he would not have met Lady Stanbury or be at this moment sitting in her house.

He dressed for dinner turning the situation over and over in his mind. He was not going to be blackmailed or made to do anything he disliked by anybody, yet he realized that he would have to use his brains where Herbert was concerned.

Undoubtedly the man was to a certain extent implicated in the business of obtaining money by false pretences, but his position was not half so dangerous as was his own. None of the women who had come to the flat had ever seen Moore or even knew he existed.

It would be difficult for him if it came to show-down, to prove Moore's partnership. The particulars of the men killed had been burned after each interview or the fact that they were in Herbert's handwriting might have been a point in his favour.

He had no intention of letting Moore expose him or the fraud in which he had participated, but he was well aware that when it came to threats Moore would hold all the winning trumps.

"I have got out of worse troubles in my life," Frank said to himself, "and I will get out of this one."

As he came down to dinner to meet the welcoming smile of Lady Stanbury and the keen searching eyes of Colonel Harrison he despised himself for being afraid.

* * *

Lady Hood took a personal interest in the men themselves, and although the hospital was always filled to capacity she managed never to make mistakes when she talked to the officers of their personal affairs.

She also retained in her memory, without reference to the nurses, medical details about each particular patient.

Frank, therefore, was not surprised when on Tuesday morning Lady Hood, pausing by his bedside, said:

"Did you enjoy your week-end, Captain Wode?"

"I had a splendid time," he answered. "Crosstrees Priory is one of the most lovely houses I have ever seen in my life."

"Yes, isn't it?" Lady Hood agreed. "I have spent some very happy days there. And how was Lady Stanbury?"

"She is wonderfully brave," Frank answered, understanding that Lady Hood referred not so much to her friend's health as to her bereavement.

153

"When you know her as well as I do you will know that Geraldine Stanbury could never be anything else. I wish there were more people like her."

"And how did your leg feel in your first absence from us?" Lady Hood added.

"It is much better," Frank said. "It's unbelievable, but I hardly ever get any pain now."

"That's splendid"; with a sweet smile she put some fruit on the table beside his bed and passed on down the ward.

When she had left him Frank lay back on his pillows. Alone again, his thoughts inevitably returned to the problems which had kept him awake the night before and to which at present he could find no solution. What was he to do about Herbert Moore?

Over and over again the telephone conversation from Crosstrees Priory repeated itself in his mind, and from what Moore had said then he was aware, both from the tone of his voice and by instinct which would not be denied, that he had a difficult task before him.

Herbert meant to blackmail him into continuing to make easy money, and he would use any means, however unsavoury and crooked, to get his own way.

Frank was not only afraid of his exposing, to the women from whom he had obtained money, the deception about his friendship with their sons; Moore was the only person in London at the moment who knew the real identity of Wyndham Wode.

He might now know the reason for his change of name, in fact Frank thought that it was unlikely that he should, but there was always the possibility of discovery.

Perhaps, he told himself, he was giving the man credit for more intelligence than he really possessed, nevertheless, enquiries were not difficult with a name to work with, and there was invariably some discreditable if not criminal reason for a man changing his identity.

But fears and anxieties could do no good. He despised himself, not merely for the part he had played in obtaining money by such methods, but in letting a man of Moore's type gain such a hold over him. He remembered Sir Alfred once saying to him:

"People don't pay for wickedness in this world, my boy, but for stupidity."

Frank saw the truth of this now, he had been absurdly stupid in entering into a partnership by which, in the event of exposure, he could be pronounced guilty without his fellow-conspirator being in any way implicated.

Dressing slowly, after he had been inspected by the surgeon, he felt tired and apprehensive of what the afternoon's interview would bring forth.

He was not so well that worry and a sleepless night did not put him back a good deal, but he dared not complain in case he was sent back to bed.

He would suffer anything rather than run the risk of Moore fulfilling his threat of coming to see him at the Home.

As he took a khaki shirt from the chest of drawers by his bedside a sudden impulse made him pick up the service revolver from where he had carelessly thrown it at the back of the drawer and slip it into his pocket.

He had not yet formulated any plan for countering Moore's threats but he felt that he might have to use desperate measures.

In the privacy of the cloakroom he loaded his revolver and somehow the weight of it in his pocket gave him a new confidence, so that when luncheon was over he set out from Carlton House Terrace with renewed courage.

As he walked up Lower Regent Street he wondered how many of the passers-by were facing tremendous issues in their daily lives.

He felt lonely, a human being struggling without a helping hand or an understanding word, yet London was not the grim, austere place he had once thought it.

155

There was a cheery good humour to be found everywhere which had not been there in 1911 and a spirit of friendship between man and man because they were linked in a common cause against an enemy.

While Frank cursed his imagination which made him sensitive to these changes, he felt ashamed.

He arrived at Herbert Moore's flat three-quarters of an hour before there was any chance of the owner being present. He let himself in with his key and walked restlessly about the small room trying to force his thoughts into some constructive channel.

He remembered now that Moore knew even the name of his bank in which the money had been deposited while he himself had no idea where Moore had put his share.

Grimly he sat down at the desk determined if possible to find out something about Moore's private life.

He was not surprised to find that all the drawers were locked and quite determinedly and without thought of what explanation he would make he forced the lock of the middle drawer.

Inside papers were stacked precisely and tidily, which was an indication of Moore's character. There were several bills and receipts, a note-book which contained household accounts for the past three months, and some sheets of stamped note-paper.

Certainly there was nothing of importance there.

Frank shut the drawer again and opened another. This was not so tidy and looked at first glance as if someone had hurriedly replaced several papers before closing the drawer.

On the top was a telegram. It was from Holland and read:

Many happy returns of the day. Love to Emily. Aunt Mary.

"I thought all Herbert's people lived in England," Frank said to himself.

He remembered the times the man had protested that

he had no relations living abroad; then above the words Frank noticed lightly pencilled numbers.

He stared at them for a moment without understanding and then it was clear—the telegram was in code.

Quickly he pulled all the other things out of the drawer until at the back he found what he sought—a small grey book which would conveniently go into a man's pocket.

Frank understood decoding but it took him nearly twenty-five minutes before finally, even with the help of the already pencilled-in numbers, he could understand the message as Herbert Moore must have read it:

Information received. Send names of regiments south of . . .

He could not make out the last word. The telegram was unsigned.

With the decoded telegram in front of him he sat staring at it, aware of what he had discovered.

Herbert Moore was a spy!

Frank realized now how credulous he had been to believe that this flat with its expensive furnishings, and the small but luxurious car which Herbert owned could have been paid for by his salary at the War Office.

In the old days Moore had been shabby, had hung round bars in the West End hoping to find someone to stand him a drink, thankful of earning a little money by any means, honest or otherwise.

"What a fool I've been!" Frank thought.

He thrust the telegram into his pocket and shutting the drawer got to his feet and went slowly into the bedroom. There were ivory brushes lying neatly on the polished walnut dressing table.

Frank opened the wardrobe and saw rows of well-cut suits. There was a picture over the mantelpiece that looked valuable and the rug beside the bed was of fine quality.

"All bought by the lives of men," Frank said to himself.

Suddenly he shuddered. The whole flat filled him with horror. He thought of Herbert Moore coming back from the War Office where he had handled those long, miserable lists of men killed, wounded, and missing.

He would sit down at his desk and send out what information he could to the country of his origin, to the country that he disclaimed so readily in public.

In a position of trust there were various ways in which he could obtain information from departments other than his own from men engaged like himself because they were unfit for military service.

"The bloody swine!" Frank said out loud to himself.

Even as he spoke there was the sound of light, jaunty footsteps coming up the stairway to the flat.

"Glad to see you, old man," Herbert said, coming into the room breezily and flinging his hat down on the chair beside the door. "Well, did you enjoy your weekend? You were lucky to catch me in on Sunday night. I was just dressing for dinner, as it happened, and if you'd been ten minutes later I should have gone out."

He crossed the room and took the whisky from the cupboard under the sideboard.

"Have a drink?" he said. "I can do with one myself and I don't suppose you'll say no."

He put the decanter down on the table, then something in Frank's silence and his attitude as he stood resting on his crutches in the centre of the room made him pause.

"What's the matter?" he asked sharply. "Don't look so glum about things. Have a drink before we start our discussion."

"No, thank you," Frank said.

"Well, just as you please," Moore replied, "but I certainly shan't be so abstemious."

He poured himself out half a tumbler of whisky, added a dash of soda and drank it off.

"I wanted that," he said, smacking his lips. "I've had a tiring morning."

"The casualty lists are heavy, then?" Frank asked bitterly.

"Terrible!" Moore answered in a grave voice.

"Terrible! And now," he said abruptly, helping himself to a cigarette from a big silver box, "suppose we sit down and have a little chat."

"About what?" Frank asked quietly.

"About yourself," Herbert answered. "When you rang me up on Sunday night I admit that I wasn't complete surprised. I had an idea that weekends in the country with smart, well-known people might make you lose your sense of proportion; in fact I was quite prepared to hear from you sooner or later."

"Really!" Frank said. "That's very interesting. Go on."

"When we went into this little business together," Moore said, studying the end of his cigarette, "I thought to myself that it seemed a pity that I should do so much work and entrust to you my idea unless I was prepared to safeguard myself in one way or another, so I made a few enquiries about you.

"At the same time, as you are doubtless aware by now, I took very good care that nothing should in any way implicate me if these little interviews should at any time be the subject of enquiries or any sort of unpleasantness."

"Yes, you were very clever," Frank said.

"I thought you'd think that."

Herbert spoke with satisfaction.

"I pride myself that when I do something I take such pecular pains with the organization of it that I seldom, if ever, have a failure.

"Well, to be quite frank with you, I am afraid, in the event of us not seeing eye to eye, that I shall have a great deal to say both to the women who entrusted you with their money and also to Lady Stanbury.

"I gather from what you said on the telephone the other night, she has offered you some position or employment with more money and perhaps more congenial than you have at the moment."

"In other words," Frank said, moving his position so that he could lean for support against the table in the centre of the room, "you intend to blackmail me."

"That's a hard word," Herbert said with a disparaging gesture. "Shall we put it this way? I think that you are being very foolish. We are on to a very good thing which so far we have hardly begun to use to the best of its possibilities.

"Why should my plans be upset because you hear of what you imagine will be better employment, although I think it's hardly likely to bring you in much more money? You must say I am at least logical."

As he received no answer, he continued:

"Now come, don't let's quarrel over this—that would be ridiculous where partners are concerned. You are behaving very stupidly and after all you need the money more than I do.

"These new friends of yours will take you up for a few weeks, then they'll find someone more interesting or more entertaining and they'll drop you like a hot brick. You'll be lucky if you're left with any sort of job when they've finished with you."

"That's all exceedingly interesting," Frank said. "And now, if you've finished all you want to say perhaps you will let me speak."

"Go ahead, my dear fellow," Moore answered. "I am sure you have a very good case and I am delighted to listen to it."

"Well, perhaps, then, you will explain this, Herman Müller," Frank said, taking the decoded telegram out of his pocket.

For a moment he thought the man was going to have a fit; he went ashen white and his hand crept chokingly to his collar as if in need of air.

Recovering himself he stepped towards Frank as though he would strike him. Frank's superior height

160

made him pause and in a voice that seemed to snarl rather than speak, he asked:

"Where did you get that?"

Frank replaced the telegram in his pocket.

"From your drawer," he answered quietly.

With an obvious effort Moore pulled himself together.

"Well, what about it?" he said. "A letter of congratulations on my birthday, which was yesterday."

"Unfortunately," Frank answered, "I've been here a long time and managed to decode your birthday wishes."

Some seconds elapsed before, with what was an almost pathetic attempt at bravado, Moore said:

"Well, we both seem to be in the same boat, after all. You can give me away if you like, in which case I shall most certainly explain your presence in the flat.

"I am not certain that in such a case you wouldn't be worse off than me. After all, I am a German fighting for my own country; that's honest at any rate and you must admit has a certain glamour about it.

"You are an Englishman obtaining money by false pretences from the mothers of sons who have been killed fighting for their King and Country—in other words, you are making money out of the war even as I am, but making it from your own side."

The strength came back into Moore's voice as he talked even as the colour was returning to his face.

He was nervous, he had had a shock, but the natural bombast of the little man was standing him in good stead. He was not as afraid as he had been. Already, with his quick scheming brain, he was trying to hypnotize Frank by words.

"I am sorry," Frank said, "but your arguments are not very convincing. Mine, at least, are going to prove more forceful."

He put his hand in his pocket and drew out his revolver.

"Get up, you little swine!" he said.

Moore stared at him in fascinated horror.

"What are you going to do?" he gasped.

"Go and sit at your desk," Frank answered.

Moore looked wildly round, but as if he realized there was no escape he got slowly to his feet.

It was quiet outside in the street and although he glanced towards the window at the noise of a passing motor he obviously thought better of making a dash in that direction.

He sat down at his desk as he was told, keeping an eye on the revolver that Frank held in his hand.

"You wouldn't dare shoot," he said shrilly, "you wouldn't dare! I defy you!"

"I shouldn't do anything of the sort," Frank said coolly. "No one knows I have come here this afternoon and you know full well the advantages of your quiet secluded little flat over a warehouse which is so seldom used. Get some writing paper."

Moore pulled open a drawer.

"Take your pen," Frank commanded, "and write this."

For a moment the man seemed on the verge of another frenzied outburst, then a look at the revolver which Frank held unpleasantly near made him obey.

"I can't bear this inaction any longer," Frank dictated. "The lists get worse every day. I can't sleep, they haunt me."

"What's this mean? What are you making me write?" Moore asked.

He had obviously expected a confession of his guilt and his expression was one of genuine surprise.

"Do as you're told," Frank answered.

Then, as Moore inscribed the last word, he bent forward and putting the barrel of the revolver against the man's temple, fired.

There was the shattering shock of the explosion, and Moore crumpled forward on to his desk.

For a moment Frank stood looking down at him, his face grim and expressionless.

Then, taking a silk handkerchief from his pocket he wiped his finger-prints from the revolver and lifting Moore's limp hand pressed the fingers on the trigger and round the barrel.

Afterwards he let the weapon fall to the floor as it might have done naturally.

Without disturbing the dead body he pulled open the drawer on the left-hand side of the desk and replaced the telegram where he had originally found it.

Carefully he wiped the handle of the drawer, the arm of the chair, and moving slowly across the room he replaced the unused glass in the sideboard, leaving the decanter and the glass from which Moore had drunk on the table.

He took a last look round, then taking his cap he put it on his head and still covering his fingers with the silk handkerchief opened the door and let himself out.

In the street he wasted no time. He moved as quickly as he could to the corner, turned down a labyrinth of small streets until finally he emerged into the crowded thoroughfare of Regent Street.

Here he hailed a taxi and told the man to drive to the Alhambra. Earlier in the day several officers at Lady Hood's had announced their intention of going to a matinée to hear once again Violet Lorraine in *The Bing Boys*.

Frank on arrival took a rover ticket. He stood in the darkness for some time until, a few minutes before the second interval would occur, he edged his way gradually towards the bar.

He was having a drink when two of the men he had expected to see came elbowing their way up to the crowded counter.

"Hello, Wode!" they exclaimed at the sight of him. "Didn't know you were coming this afternoon."

163

"I changed my mind," Frank answered, "and I'm glad I did. She's up to her usual form, isn't she?"

"By Jove, she's a marvel!" was the reply. "And I think George is funnier than ever this afternoon, don't you?"

"If they don't Knight him at the end of the war they damn' well ought to!" the other man said, adding: "Here, your glass is empty. Have one with me."

When the curtain rose they went back together, and at the end of the show shared a taxi to Carlton House Terrace.

Only when he undressed that evening did Frank wonder whether there was any chance of his revolver being identified, but he felt that the authorities would not be eager to attribute the suicide of a German spy to murder.

After all, there was every likelihood of them wanting to hush up the fact that such a man had for the last few years held a position of trust in the War Office.

Frank was surprised to notice how calm he was and how unagitated, even when the evening papers were brought to the ward.

It was ridiculous to think there might be anything in them, yet the thought crossed his mind. He waited quietly, however, until he was able to obtain one.

Only when the lights were out and the sound of quiet breathing from the other beds told him that the occupants were sleeping did he lie with wide eyes staring into the darkness and question himself as to whether he had done right.

A second question which forced itself upon his consciousness was—what had been his true motive? Had he shot Herbert Moore because he was a spy, or because he was being blackmailed by him?

He tried to divorce the two problems. How had he intended originally to deal with the blackmailer? What would he have done if he had discovered the man to be a spy and had had no other dealings with him?

"Damn' it! I'm getting introspective," Frank told himself.

But he could not sleep and again and again the questions presented themselves until he felt that to have any peace he must find the answer to them.

"Am I a coward?" he asked himself. "And am I a murderer?"

Taking life had seemed so unimportant in France, yet because he had shot a man in cold blood sitting at his desk it preyed on his mind.

Even when he had been one of a firing-squad he had gone away afterwards to eat a hearty breakfast and to forget the whole thing in a few hours.

He remembered the terror on Herbert Moore's face when he had first produced the revolver. In a way the little man had been brave to undertake such a job. Whatever the remuneration, he had known that the penalty of discovery was death.

He must have thought himself singularly safe in his compact little flat where only a charwoman went, who cleaned the place in the mornings.

She would discover him tomorrow, Frank thought. If Moore had made some appointment with a friend for this evening they would probably hammer on the door, ring the bell, and getting no answer think there had been some mistake and go away.

Frank remembered the men he had seen dead and dying in the front line in France.

Vividly their faces came back to him: the upturned eyes, the dropped jaw, perhaps a crimson tide of blood flowing down from a wound in the forehead.

In the darkness of the ward he told himself fiercely that he was glad he had killed their betrayer.

CHAPTER TEN

Frank arranged his luggage in the compartment, spreading it over the seats in the hope that fellow-passengers would think that they were engaged and would not disturb him.

Already his journey had been delayed and he had missed his first connection from Paris. It was to be expected in war time, however; several times they had been shunted into a siding while troop trains went past.

Frank thought of the discomfort, the crowded carriages, and the lack of food on those long trains carrying men to the front line.

The German push south of Paris had failed, but reinforcements were being rapidly massed there.

Frank's train had been comparatively empty, but he found it singularly difficult to travel as a civilian *en route* for Switzerland.

In spite of the facilities given him before he left England he was continually being interrogated, having his luggage searched, and finding that fresh permits were necessary before he could proceed.

Colonel Harrison had, however, warned him to expect this and he took all that came to him with a good humour that made things easier than if he had, as did some of the other passengers on the train, given vent to his irritation and sense of injustice.

He felt well, although it was only three weeks since he had received his discharge from the Army; which had been hastened behind the scenes by Colonel Harrison.

When he left Lady Hood's hospital he had been invited to Crosstrees Priory and spent nearly a fortnight there before coming to London for an interview with the Colonel.

His stay at Crosstrees had been not only good for his health, but mentally and spiritually he felt himself to be a different man after his visit. He had gone there troubled in mind.

There was no reason for him to be nervous, for a few lines in the papers was the only obituary notice that Herbert Moore received.

The coroner at the inquest had merely remarked that his work in the casualty department and the fact that he was unfit to serve in the Army had caused him to take his life while of unsound mind.

Although Frank was free from the fear of disclosure, he found himself since that eventful afternoon thinking more deeply and seriously than he had ever done in his life before.

All that had happened to him in the past, even the years of war, seemed hardly to have impressed him, but the murder of Moore combined with the advent into his life of Lady Stanbury had somehow altered and changed him.

For the first time he asked himself where he was drifting, what the urge by which he had been spurred on ever since he was twenty-two meant, whether it had any roots or was merely frivolous desire for change and escape.

He wanted to know more about himself, about his own character, about his own strivings.

"What have I achieved?" Frank asked himself dispassionately.

To every man at some time in his life there comes a

moment of self-revelation; to Frank this now meant nights of sleeplessness and days of depression.

His confidence left him and he felt that he stood naked in a strange world, ashamed and humbled.

But at Crosstrees Priory he felt the stirring of a new spirit, which brought him new hope.

They were a small party this time, Lady Stanbury and two old friends of hers, a married couple who like herself had lost their only son in the war.

"I have not asked any young people to meet you," she said to Frank when she had welcomed him. "I thought you would like a quiet time and a real rest before you start on your work."

Frank had not questioned her as to what this work would be; he was sufficiently wise to understand that when the moment arrived and Colonel Harrison wanted him he would be sent for.

In the meantime it was his duty to get fit and strong and to reserve all his mental efforts for what lay before him.

The gardens of the Priory were at their very best and Frank lay under the trees or wandered slowly across the lawns feeling the country air and sunshine bring back to him his joy of life.

One Saturday morning he saw Lady Stanbury coming from the house carrying a huge basket of lilies.

"I'm going to do the flowers for the church," she said. "Would you like to come with me?"

Frank got to his feet eagerly. Every moment that he spent alone with his hostess he found of interest and of encouragement.

He genuinely loved her, and there was in her very presence an inspiration which transmitted itself to everyone with whom she came in contact.

They moved slowly towards the little grey stone church which was only a short distance from the house. Frank noticed that the churchyard was beautifully tended and that there were flowers on nearly all the graves, either growing or freshly arranged in vases.

Through the oak-arched porch they entered into the cool dimness of the aisle which was carpeted so that their footsteps did not disturb the peace of the building itself.

When she had finished and they turned again towards the house, Frank said to her:

"I wonder why you have been so kind to me?"

Lady Stanbury paused for a moment before she answered.

"I think perhaps you are in need of kindness," she said.

"What makes you say that?" Frank asked.

She did not reply directly to his question, but asked him:

"Am I not right?"

"I think perhaps you are," Frank said. "And yet if I am honest I should say I wasn't conscious of it myself until I first came here. Your life and the world in which you live are so very different from anything I have ever known before; but I think that this is what I have unconsciously been seeking."

Lady Stanbury shook her head.

"No," she said, "you are wrong. You think that because you have been ill and because you don't yet feel strong enough to face the daily battle which is the lot of every man who works. This place is too restful, too quiet.

"It is a haven for those who have reached the last years of their life, like myself. There are big things for you to do yet, important things, and I wonder if you realize that."

She paused a moment and then she added:

"By things of importance I don't mean from a worldly point of view, I mean for yourself. Every one of us sooner or later has to find ourselves and to reach out for our own highest standard."

"During these past few weeks," Frank said, "I have realized how utterly I have failed to do that very thing, but I wasn't aware until now that I had a standard."

"There can be no possibility of happiness for any of us," Lady Stanbury said, "until we know what we are going to demand of life and how we intend to get it."

"Isn't that rather selfish?" Frank asked.

"If your demands are selfish naturally it will be so," she replied, "but I think the whole trouble with our up-bringing, is that we look upon 'being good' as non-doing instead of as action. Only by active development in the right direction can we ever achieve anything."

"Actions are always dangerous," Frank said. "One seldom knows when one does them if they are good or bad, especially when another person is involved."

"I firmly believe," Lady Stanbury replied, "that if we do anything that is evil it must sooner or later be expiated by us, either in this life or in another one; in fact our debts accumulate until we can pay them."

"I wonder?" Frank murmured.

He thought of the people he had hurt in his life—Helga, Edith, other women who had turned from him with tears and reproaches, men he had swindled, friends he had let down. . .

"But that surely is hell?" he said suddenly, and Lady Stanbury replied quietly:

"Why not? We make our own heaven and hell."

They had further talks during his visit and always he was struck by the sanity of her philosophy and the simplicity of her faith.

Perhaps Lady Stanbury was the only person of Frank's acquaintance to realize how young in many ways he still was.

He had a natural ability and a retentive and astute intellect, but in some respects he was undeveloped. He had no idea of his own possibilities.

The more she associated with him and as she grew to know him better, Lady Stanbury told herself that her instinct had been right when, in the first moment that she met Frank, she had thought that here was a man worth cultivating—raw material, perhaps, but genuine.

* * *

Frank, sitting in the train, opened his small despatch-case and looked at some snapshots taken at Crosstrees Priory.

The sunshine glinted on the casement windows and showed up its black-and-white beauty as it stood silhouetted against a dark background of trees.

For him it symbolized all that was best in England.

His interview with Colonel Harrison had been surprising. The Colonel had spoken shortly with a brevity of words which was characteristic of him.

He had told Frank what his mission was to be, handed him certain documents—among them a code which he was to commit to memory—then shaking him warmly by the hand had shown him to the door.

Frank was almost bewildered with the quickness of it all. Before he knew where he was he had obeyed orders, bought clothes and packed them, purchased a ticket to Switzerland through the ordinary agency and set out for St. Wolfe.

"There is information being passed through a German post of some sort in that neighbourhood," Colonel Harrison had said. "It is one of many, of course; one of our chief difficulties at the moment is to check up in any way on the Swiss frontier, but if we find out who is the transmitter that in itself generally leads us to the people who provide the information.

"There is an hotel at St. Wolfe which remains open all the year round chiefly for the convenience of invalids.

"You will go there to convalesce, stating quite frankly that you are an officer recently discharged from the British Army and using your right name.

"You will allay suspicion by your frankness, and your interest in your fellow-guests will be a friendly and natural one.

"You may find the suspected person to be a man or woman staying in the hotel, a waiter, or a shopkeeper in the district. In many cases an Englishman married to a German wife or the other way about turns out to be the person we want, but that is for you to discover.

"I can give you no lead and no clue for we have none. As soon as you are certain who the person is you will send a telegram in code to this address in Savile Row.

"To all intents and purposes it will read as an instruction to your tailor about a new suit. You will then await further orders from me, which in all probability will be to return home.

"Confide in no one, trust no one, and commit everything to memory. Is that quite clear?"

"Yes, sir," Frank answered.

"If you will give me the name of your bankers money will be paid in to cover the expenses of the journey. There will be no need for you to acknowledge it.

"You mustn't get into any trouble of any sort with the authorities. That, I presume, is perfectly clear. If you do you will receive no help from us, in fact we shall deny all knowledge of you."

"I understand," Frank answered.

"Good-bye," Colonel Harrison said, holding out his hand, and smiling, he added: "Good luck, Wode."

Frank felt that he was embarking on an adventure as he set off two days later from Victoria Station with a miscellaneous collection of civilian travellers.

He amused himself by trying to recognize what type of men they were from their appearance and trying to guess their occupation.

He arrived at St. Wolfe very late the following evening. Although the day had been one of brilliant sun-

172

shine and great heat the night was cool with a touch of ice in the air which came from distant glaciers.

As he stepped out at the small wayside station and collected his luggage around him Frank heard the torrential sound of water flowing down the mountainside, and smelt the sweet fragrant scent of many flowers.

The porter carried his luggage to the one vehicle which waited outside the station, a somewhat dilapidated bus which he was informed would put him down at his hotel.

He climbed into it, seating himself beside a pretty rosy-cheeked girl who held firmly with one hand the bound feet of a white cockerel and with the other clasped the arm of a burly sunburnt young man.

Two or three villagers who had come to the station for parcels climbed into the motor.

Frank's luggage was hoisted on top, and they set off, running down the narrow dusty roadway to where, far away in the distance, shone the yellow twinkling lights of St. Wolfe.

An old lady in the corner dropped her chin on her voluminous chest and shut her eyes; a man with a long moustache took out his pipe and spat reflectively out of the back window; the young couple whispered and giggled together.

Only Frank stared out into the darkness; as they came nearer to his destination he felt his heart beating excitedly in anticipation of what might be before him.

* * *

The sunshine, coming through the dining-room window, glinted on the coffee-pot, the knives and plated salt-cellars, in almost dazzling fashion.

Frank stared out at the view which lay before him and let his breakfast grow cold because of its loveliness.

He had never believed that any place could be so beautiful or that the sides of mountains could show such

173

a profusion of wild flowers while their peaks were still white with snow.

It was with difficulty that he could take his eyes from the panorama outside and inspect his fellow-breakfasters. He had come down early for that very purpose; besides he had not been able to sleep.

He felt a little lonely at his corner table and was glad to pass the time of day with the waiter, who spoke perfect English and informed him that five years ago he had been working at the Savoy in London.

He asked Frank several questions about the restaurant and told him that he had spent his free time in London at the Zoo, which he considered one of the marvels of modern civilization.

He was a pale-faced little man of about thirty-five with three gold teeth and an untidy mop of fair hair which had obviously been cut by the village barber.

He seemed genuinely anxious to please and Frank felt that here was someone likely to help him with his investigations.

"Are there many people staying in the hotel?" he asked.

"Not very many," the waiter replied. "We have had a bad season. People find it difficult to get here and many of our old clients are either fighting or have no money left for holidays."

Frank did not like to ask too many questions at once; the average Englishman was generally indifferent to his fellows, so he allowed the conversation to lapse as he poured out a second cup of coffee.

At the far end of the room a large, fat woman who looked French was accompanied by a sallow-skinned girl of about nineteen.

They ate their breakfast in silence, the older woman reading a newspaper, the girl keeping her eyes on her plate and taking no interest in anything else.

Frank and the two women were at first the only people present, then the door opened to admit an elderly man leading an ancient Aberdeen terrier and followed by his wife limping on two sticks.

Frank remembered Colonel Harrison's words about an Englishman married to a German wife; the elderly man was obviously English.

Frank judged that in all probability he had spent part of his life abroad, he had the type of tough, weather-beaten complexion which seems essentially to belong to Anglo-Indians or inhabitants of our outposts of Empire.

Immediately upon arriving at his table he ordered the waiter to close the window above it, speaking in the loud commanding voice of a man who was used to authority.

Frank looked at his wife with interest, but when he heard her speak, as somewhat peevishly she sent back the breakfast-roll as being too hard, he put down her accent as the most refined Kensington and certainly not of any nationality other than British.

After breakfast Frank went for a stroll. At the end of the street he turned to retrace his steps and saw coming towards him a tall, athletic-looking man with grey hair.

As they met the man hesitated for a moment, then said:

"Were you looking for the club, by any chance? It's the next turning farther down, you know."

"I wasn't," Frank answered, "but thank you all the same. In fact, I didn't know there was a club."

The man laughed.

"I saw you arrive last night," he confessed, "and generally that's the first thing we English people ask for. It's a snug little hole as a rule, but empty this year, of course. The tennis-courts are fair and there's quite a sporty golf-course."

"I'm afraid neither are much use to me at the moment," Frank replied, "but I'd like to join, all the same, if I'm allowed to."

"Oh, there'll be no difficulty about that. Come along

with me and I'll put you up. As it happens guests at the hotel are elected almost automatically."

"It's very good of you," Frank said.

"Not at all," was the answer, "and by the way, I'd better introduce myself. My name's Loder, George Loder."

"And mine is Wyndham Wode," Frank said.

"I must confess I knew that," was the answer. "I'm afraid you will think we are very curious, but a newcomer is always an excitement to us habitués."

"You live here, then?" Frank asked.

"Yes, all the year round," the other replied. "My wife's an invalid and the doctors say her only chance of remaining alive is to stay permanently in this air. Of course I shouldn't be here at the moment if I wasn't over age. I'd like to have done my bit the same as the rest of you."

Frank cynically wondered if he spoke the truth. George Loder was not a young man, at the same time since the age limit had been raised he thought from appearances there was a likelihood of his being eligible.

He wondered about the invalid wife, for this seemed to him the very type that Colonel Harrison had told him to be on the look-out for. He decided not to appear too curious; whatever happened he must not put Loder on his guard.

"I'm out here to convalesce," he volunteered.

"I gathered that was your reason," Loder replied. "Did you have a bad time?"

"Pretty rotten," Frank answered. "Shell wounds in the leg."

The other man looked appropriately sympathetic.

"Well, this place will soon put you on your feet," he said. "The air here is wonderful, you'll feel a different person in a day or two. How long are you staying?"

"I really don't know," Frank answered. "There's no hurry for me now; I was given my discharge a few weeks ago."

"Oh, then you're your own master again," Loder said. "Well, you've certainly done your bit. God knows I wish I could say the same!"

Frank grew more suspicious of him as he continually harped on his desire to fight.

He remembered how Herbert Moore was always bewailing his fate at being unfit and this seemed to Frank a parallel instance.

He thought with satisfaction that Colonel Harrison would be pleased with him if so shortly after his arrival he was on the right track; yet it behooved him to go as slowly as possible and not to make a false step.

When they got to the club-house he was introduced to the secretary, a small frightened-looking Swiss with glasses who agreed hurriedly with everything that Mr. Loder suggested, then they repaired to the bar.

They had a drink together and while they were still drinking the secretary came hurrying in to say that Loder's partner for the morning round was waiting for him at the first tee.

"Well, I must be off," he said, rising to his feet. "I shall see you later."

"That'll be awfully nice," Frank answered. "And thank you very much for all you've done."

Frank went back to the hotel for luncheon thinking he had done a good morning's work.

He wished in some ways that he could report daily progress to Colonel Harrison, but he knew that on no account was he to communicate with him until he was completely certain and a telegram with the definite information required could be despatched to Savile Row.

As he entered the hall he met the postman carrying a bulging bag of letters, and with several parcels suspended from his shoulders. The proprietor was sorting out the correspondence for his guests, marking the number of each room on the letters.

"Anything for me?" Frank asked, leaning over the reception-desk.

"Nothing, *mein Herr*."

After luncheon Frank went up to his bedroom and unpacked some of the books he had brought with him. Two or three of them had been given to him by Lady Stanbury, the rest had been of her recommendation and he had purchased them before leaving London.

He chose one at random, but when he was finally seated beside his open window he found his thoughts wandering and was unable to concentrate.

It seemed ridiculous to think that George Loder might be a spy transmitting slips of information received from many different agents over the frontier into Germany.

It was easy enough to do and Frank knew as Colonel Harrison had told him that it was being done in innumerable places in Switzerland; yet he failed to understand how any Englishman could want to mix himself up in such a dirty, degrading business.

Supposing Loder was the man he was searching for, Frank wondered what Colonel Harrison's methods would be when the information reached him? How would Loder be dealt with? he asked himself.

There was a ruthlessness and a quiet determination about David Harrison which made Frank believe that whatever methods he employed they would be effective.

There was also the possibility that Harrison might keep him here using him as a purveyor of false information while the real material was intercepted.

If the other side found out that Loder was betraying them he would have little chance of mercy.

Even allowing for the exaggeration of propaganda against German brutality, he had seen enough of the prisoners in France to realize that they were genuinely terrified by those in command.

He dozed a little as the afternoon passed by and the sun sank lower behind the mountains.

He roused himself with a start to find that it was long

past tea-time and he had only a short time before he was to meet Loder again for a drink.

He went downstairs and he came out on to the terrace to find that Loder was already there and that by his side, lying languidly back against cushions with her raised legs wrapped in a rug, was the woman who was obviously his wife.

"Ah, here you are, Wode!" Loder shouted. "We are waiting for you and I have ordered you something worthy of the occasion. My dear," he said, turning to the lady by his side, "Captain Wode."

Frank held out his hand.

"How do you do, Mrs. Loder?" he said. "Your husband has been exceedingly kind to me already."

"George is always so pleased to be of use," was the answer, and Frank's hopes were dashed as he realized that Mrs. Loder was certainly not of German nationality.

He sat down beside her and listened to her husband as he launched into a long, uninteresting description of his prowess on the links.

Frank felt his suspicions of Loder oozing away. If there was no doubt of Mrs. Loder's adoration, Loder was just as apparently pleased with her.

He interrupted his story several times to ask if she were comfortable, and once he touched her hand in a manner which left no doubt as to the genuineness of the affection which lay behind the gesture.

Here, then, was the explanation of Loder shirking from active service, and one certainly more compatible with the man's character than any other.

He loved his wife, his wife loved him; she was frail and in all probability it was true that she would be unable to live anywhere except in this rarefied air.

He had chosen a coward's course, but, like many better men, he had chosen it with the excuse of love.

Frank sighed as he picked up his cocktail-glass and drained it.

He had an uneasy conviction that his mission was not going to be as simple as he had optimistically believed earlier in the day.

* * *

The Loders had been invaluable, in that they were a mine of information about everyone in the place.

They knew all the shop people and the history of their families; here again Frank drew a blank, though for twenty-four hours he had been strongly suspicious of a Swiss doctor.

"A liqueur, darling?" George Loder said to his wife as they all sat outside on the terrace.

He helped her into a low deck-chair and lifted her legs on to a stool, that was brought out especially for her from the dining-room.

"Not for me," she answered, smiling at him.

"Then what about you, Wode?" he asked.

"I'll keep you company," Frank replied.

Loder's voice echoed over the terrace shouting for the waiter.

Suddenly a movement on the floor above the dining-room caught Frank's eye. A woman had been standing on the balcony overlooking the terrace; she went in now through the long french window, shutting it behind her.

Frank turned too late to see her face, but the glimpse he had of her told him that here was someone he had not seen before.

He remembered that the first day he had noticed the first-floor suite was occupied.

"Who is in the rooms over the dining-room?" he asked, turning to Mrs. Loder. "Don't they come down to meals?"

Mrs. Loder shook her head.

"No," she answered. "She used to when she first arrived. She actually tried to be friendly but we and several other people made our feelings very clear, so now she stays in her own room."

"Hardly ever comes out," said George, "except in the evening. I've met her walking down to the post-office several times when I was coming back from the club. Damned awkward, in a way, meeting her face to face."

"Why, what's wrong with her?" Frank asked, full of curiosity.

George lowered his voice a little.

"She's a Hun," he said shortly.

"What makes it worse"—Mrs. Loder took up the tale—"she's married to an Englishman called Caylor. Of course we don't know, in fact I've no right to say so, but we think it very suspicious that she should be here in Switzerland while apparently he is fighting in France."

"I don't think you need worry," Frank said with a smile. "Our censorship's pretty strict, you know, they don't take many chances with letters from the front line, at any rate."

Although he spoke casually he felt excited. Here, at last, might be the person he was looking for, a German woman married to an English husband; it fitted in well with Colonel Harrison's expectations.

When Frank left the Loders he went slowly to his bedroom. His immediate problem was to get to know Mrs. Caylor, and he cursed himself for having wasted five days at St. Wolfe without having realized that the occupant of that suite might be the very person he had come here to find.

To pick up an acquaintanceship with a woman who never appeared was a difficult task.

Even if he hung about the street in the hope of meeting her after dark he could hardly walk up to a complete stranger who obviously preferred seclusion, and say:

"Excuse me, but can I talk to you?"

When he reached his own bedroom he sat down by the window.

"I am not going to fail," Frank told himself.

He realized that this, his first job, had been given to him as a trial.

Colonel Harrison, in their talk together, had made no promises for the future, in fact he had spoken as if Frank was an entirely free agent to go on or not as he pleased once the preliminary step was past.

He put out his hand, took a cigarette from the small table beside him and lit it.

He let the match burn down towards his fingers and then with a flick of his thumb spun it in the air so that it sped through the open window. As he watched it disappear an idea came to him.

He rose to his feet as quickly as he was able to do so and leant over the window-sill. As he looked below he realized that he had found the solution to his problem.

The balcony of Mrs. Caylor's suite ran directly beneath his own windows.

Frank stood for a moment deliberating; he picked up one of his books. He turned over the pages and then replaced it tidily with the others before choosing another.

He was still not satisfied—a book can provide a topic of conversation—and it was nearly five minutes before he finally carried to the window-sill a weighty volume on modern art.

A German woman, he argued, would not be likely to read English novels and although there was a chance that she was interested in philosophy he must not bank on it.

Art was a neutral ground on which they could talk quite easily; everyone, he thought to himself, especially a woman, had ideas on decoration.

He opened the book, bent it back, and with a shove sent it toppling over the window-ledge. He heard it crash on to the balcony below.

He did not wait to see where it had fallen, but taking up his crutches hurried from the room and down the short flight of stairs to the next landing.

He could not run the risk of a waiter being sent to return his property before he had time to claim it.

He was breathless both with excitement and the speed of his coming downstairs when he knocked at the door of the suite.

There was a moment before anyone answered him; he had a sudden fear that luck had deserted him and that Mrs. Caylor had broken her usual rule and gone out.

Then a woman's voice answered him in German.

"Come in," she said.

He went in and found himself in a small dark hall, but the door to the sitting-room was half open and he could see a woman lying on a sofa by the window.

He pushed open the second door and entered.

"I am so sorry," he said, "but I am afraid I have dropped my book on to your balcony."

The woman was sewing; she took a further stitch before she raised her head and looked at him.

Frank had an impression of wide blue eyes, the glint of sunshine on very golden hair . . . suddenly it seemed to him as if his heart had stopped beating.

He stood, unable to move, unable to speak . . . for there looking at him was Helga.

For a moment she did not recognize him, then his expression and his stillness held her attention.

She stared at him, motionless, before with a little cry, she sprang to her feet.

"Frank!" she exclaimed. "Frank! Oh, my dear, it can't be true!"

She ran towards him and stood looking up into his face with an expression of utter bewilderment.

"It isn't true!" she repeated again.

"Helga," Frank whispered. "Helga."

He could not raise his voice, could not force it through his dry lips.

He dropped one of his crutches to the ground, put out his hand and almost fiercely gripped her arm as though to convince himself that she was real, was flesh and blood and not some mirage of his imagination.

"You are hurt," she said, "you've been wounded."

They stood looking at each other speechless, until Helga, recovering her composure, said:

"Come and sit down. You look pale. Are you all right? Can I get you something?"

Her voice was breathless.

Frank walked a few steps to a chair. As he sat down he was aware that he was shaking all over, his hands trembling.

He had never expected this, never in his wildest dreams had he thought of finding Helga. He was unnerved.

He could only stare at her in silence as she went to the sideboard at the corner of the room and bringing out a small bottle of brandy poured some into a wineglass and handed it to him.

"Drink it," she said.

She touched his shoulder in passing; then she sat down on the low sofa.

She was lovelier than ever, Frank told himself. She was thinner, which made her eyes larger, and perhaps it was the illusion of the clothes which fashion had altered so greatly since 1911, she appeared younger.

Her hair was no longer bound by a heavy plait, but was cut short with tiny natural curls bunched over her ears, a big golden wave sweeping her white forehead.

"I had no idea," Frank said at last, "that you were here."

Helga gave a little laugh that was very near to tears.

"That's obvious, my dear," she answered. "I think you are even more surprised than I am."

Frank reached out towards her.

"Give me your hand," he commanded. "I must know that you are real. I still can't believe it."

She laughed again and did as she was told. As their hands met it seemed as if the old electricity which had run between them, passionately overwhelming them in the past, was resuscitated.

Helga's hand was smooth and white in his brown one. He looked at it for a moment, then raised it to his lips.

"Had you forgotten me?" he asked.

"You know I hadn't," Helga replied. "And you?"

Frank did not answer her question for the moment, his eyes were on her hand and he clasped it gently with both of his.

"Why did you run away without a word?" he asked.

Abruptly Helga took her hand from his and rose to her feet. She went towards the window.

"I don't believe even now," she said, after nearly a minute's silence, "that I can put into words what I felt that day at Wentworth Hall. I was being torn slowly to pieces.

"When I left you I had only one idea in my head and that was never to see you again. Not because I hated you, but because I was afraid."

She turned to face him and there was a smile on her lips, though there were tears in her eyes.

"Oh, Frank," she said simply, "I loved you so desperately!"

Frank could not answer, could only look at her in silence.

"I want you to tell me everything you've been doing these past years," Helga said after a moment. "I've got so much to hear, haven't I?"

"First of all I want to hear about you," he said.

Helga shook her head.

"It's all very uninteresting, honestly."

"Not to me," he said.

Helga made a movement as though she would deliberately brush aside the emotion in his voice.

"Women's lives are always frivolous and of no account," she said brightly.

Frank looked at her with puzzled eyes. Helga was acting a part; this forced gaiety, this light chatter, were assumed. In their first few moments together she had been herself, unchanged and natural.

Carefully he watched her as he said:

"I am out here to get well. As you see, I have been badly wounded and I am convalescing. Why are you here?"

He could not prevent his voice from altering as he added:

"You've married, I understand, and to an Englishman."

"Who told you that?" Helga asked.

"People in the hotel," Frank replied.

"Yes, it's true," she said. "I have been married nearly five years, although I haven't seen my husband since the first few months after the war started. We had been travelling before that, all over the place, China, America, the West Indies.

"When war was declared he made up his mind to go to England and I came to Switzerland. I have lived in this country ever since, although I only discovered St. Wolfe about three months ago. It's a sweet little place, isn't it?"

"And your husband?" Frank asked.

"When I last heard from him he was at the front," Helga replied.

"Helga," Frank said suddenly, "give me your hand again."

Wonderingly she did so. He bent forward in his chair and reached out to take the other; he held them firmly between his.

"Look at me," he commanded.

She put back her head and he saw the deep blue of her eyes; in the black pupils he was microscopically reflected.

"Tell me the truth," he demanded, and his voice was low and urgent. "Do you love this man?"

Frank sensed rather than heard the denial that quivered for a moment on her lips before with a desperate gesture she wrenched herself free from him, turning her eyes from his.

"Of course," she answered, "why shouldn't I love my husband? Teddy is a very charming person, I assure you."

But Frank had read in her eyes the answer he required; he knew that she lied.

CHAPTER ELEVEN

The waiter cleared away the coffee-cups, brushed a few imaginary crumbs from the table with the napkin he carried under his arm, and withdrew from the room.

Helga rose and walking to the window pulled it to, to shut out the night air which had already grown chill. She switched on three rose-shaded electric lights and turned to Frank with a smile.

"Bring your cigar over here," she said. "It's much more comfortable."

She was wearing a dress of deep-blue chiffon with a bunch of crimson roses at her breast.

She looked very lovely as she settled herself against the silk cushions on the sofa.

Frank, sitting down beside her with his bad leg stretched out in front of him, wondered, as he had been wondering all the evening, if he would ever find out the truth about her.

He had a feeling that Helga was evading him, she was not natural either in her conversation or in herself.

She was amusing, she was gay, she held him spellbound as she had always done, yet all the time he was conscious of a false note, of something not quite genuine in what she said and did.

They had talked of many things. Already Frank had told her of his marriage to Edith, of his flight to Canada, of his life there in a new country, and of his return to England.

Helga had listened to him—only in repose did he feel that she was not pretending.

Of herself she had said little and when he pressed her she seemed always to elude him, to change the subject or to force some confidence from him rather than speak herself.

Of her husband she had told him nothing, yet Frank, ridiculous though it seemed, felt a deep jealous hatred of this unknown man whose name she bore.

In that self-revealing moment when Helga's eyes had told him what her lips dared not say, that she did not love the man she had married, he had felt a wild triumph.

It had been a pleasure which in its intensity was almost a pain, and he had known then that his love for Helga was as strong as it had ever been.

It had lain dormant all through these years, but it was there nevertheless, a part of him which he could not deny. He loved her and the years which had separated them seemed now unimportant and too trivial to be remembered.

He watched her, and as in the past, everything she did thrilled and surprised him.

She was so innately graceful.

There was something in her lissom movements, in the mere gesture of her long fingers or in the soft curve of her shoulder which fired him and made him long to touch her, to pour out again the words of love that trembled on his lips.

Yet he controlled himself because there was some barrier between them.

Every now and then Helga could not meet his eyes, deliberately turning away from him, avoiding his questions or answering him untruthfully.

What was it? Frank asked himself, and knew that he must know, he had to find out.

Looking at her with her golden head bent back against the cushions, the fingers of one white hand uncurled like a lotus-flower in her lap, he had a desire to seize her in his arms, to bruise her with his kisses, to demand from her passionately and brutally the truth.

Instead, flicking his cigar-ash deliberately into a glass ash-tray he said:

"Talk to me, Helga."

"What about?" she asked.

"Is there really any need for you to ask that?" Frank replied. "You know what I want to hear. Start from the beginning, or at least what was rather the end for us."

She hesitated, and he said:

"You'll have to tell me sooner or later. Let's get it over and then we can banish the past and think of the future."

She looked at him quickly out of the corner of her eyes and he had an impression that for the moment she was afraid.

"I went to Germany," she said, "you know that."

"I know you told Sir Alfred so, in the letter you left for him," Frank answered.

"Well, it was true," she said. "I had nowhere else to go. I was afraid of staying in London, and I knew little about the rest of England. I wrote the note before I left Wentworth Hall, and all the way back in the train I tried to think of some better solution, but there wasn't one.

"I didn't want to face my relations; you see, I felt quite certain that my friends would have forgotten me, and of course they had. However, I had no alternative.

"When I got back to Park Lane, Edith had gone to bed; I packed everything I possessed. Luckily I had some money, enough anyway for the journey."

"Sir Alfred hoped day after day that you would write and tell him where you were and what you were doing," Frank said.

"I had nothing to tell," Helga answered. "When I got

back to Berlin I went to my cousins, who were not too pleased to see me. They had daughters of their own and financial troubles. I stayed with them a very short time while I sought for employment.

"I got it in a typewriting office and from there I became the secretary to Baron Hostzal. I think those months in Berlin were some of the most miserable I have ever spent in the whole of my life.

"I was so utterly alone, so unhappy, and so bitterly afraid of the future. I had saved a little money in England which the bank sent me, but I knew quite well it would only last me a short time.

"Berlin was not as progressive as London, there were not nearly so many opportunities of work for women. Things were prosperous but there were plenty of men seeking employment and every job that I tried to get was out of the question because I was a woman. I was in despair.

"I was too proud to seek out the many people I had known in my father's time. A great many of them had suffered because of him, and others had forgotten my existence.

"I used to think of you during those days and remember how you had told me that at times you had been near to starvation.

"One night I walked up and down the streets wondering if I dared sell myself, but I was too much of a coward even to do that."

"Oh, my darling!" Frank whispered, but Helga seemed not to hear him.

She was staring in front of her and he saw that she was living again those terrible despairing months.

"At last my luck changed," she said. "They told me that Baron Hostzal was seeking a private secretary. Vaguely I knew the name, but I could not place him. I went to his house, a large magnificent place with footmen in livery and powdered hair to open the doors.

"I was kept waiting nearly an hour in an ante-room

before the Baron could see me. It was then I remembered who he was—a newspaper proprietor who had caused a sensation in Berlin some years before I came to England by producing a very modern and outspoken daily paper.

"Everyone had expected him to fail, but the paper caught on, it began to sell all over Germany. Its politics were as frank as its humour. The Baron was clever enough, while he was revolutionary in some of his ideas to appeal to the taste of the average middle-class family in Germany.

"There was something for everyone, and while the Government raged when he opposed them and made fun of them, the mass of the people continued to buy the paper.

"I expected to find a big, determined man, the physical embodiment in fact of his courage and audacity; instead when I was shown into the huge sombre library I thought at first there was no one present.

"I looked round in surprise before I perceived sitting in a big armchair in front of the fire, a little old man smoking a pipe. I say old because he seemed old to me; at that moment actually the Baron was not more than fifty-eight.

"He had very little hair and what remained was white, and his dark bushy eyebrows almost hid the sharpest, most intelligent grey eyes I have ever seen in a human being.

He was clean-shaven and immaculately dressed; later I learnt that he was fastidious about his clothes to the point of dandyism.

" 'So you are Fräulein Hildergard,' he said.

"His voice was quiet but surprisingly enough there was a twinkling mercurial quality about it which made everything he said seem alive and important.

" 'Yes, Baron,' I replied. 'I understand you are requiring a secretary and I would like to offer myself for the post.'

" 'I don't approve of women working,' he answered.

" 'Nor do I', I said, 'but unfortunately I have to eat.'

"He glanced at me in surprise; then he laughed, a sharp staccato laugh which was like the bark of a dog.

" 'What are your qualifications?'

"I handed him my credentials from the typing bureau which had employed me and told him that I had also been in England for several years.

" 'Why did you leave?' he asked abruptly, and, Frank, I don't know why, but I told him the truth. He was such an unusual, unexpected little man, somehow I could not lie to him, I could not make up the usual story about wanting to come back to Germany or finding the post difficult. And so I said quite simply, without really considering my answer:

" 'I was in love.'

"The Baron looked at me for a long time under his eyebrows. I was afraid, yet I felt he appreciated my frankness. I was to learn later that he was the type of man who always liked to know everything about everybody.

"Even the most personal and intimate details of someone with whom he came in contact were remembered and retained in what was a super-normal memory.

" 'Sit down,' he said to me at length, 'and take this down.'

"Fortunately I had a note-book with me. I opened it. He dictated with hardly a pause a short newspaper article, concise, vivid, and to the point. When I had finished he told me to read it back to him.

"As I came to the end he stood up, pressed a bell, and almost immediately the door was opened by a footman.

" 'Show Fräulein Hildegard to the secretary's room,' he said. To me he added: 'Despatch that article by messenger to the editor. I shall require you at two o'clock.'

"I was engaged! I left the room, Frank, walking on

193

air, I could hardly believe my good luck. I wanted to sing, to dance, to cry out. At last I had work, for the moment I was safe."

Helga clasped her hands together.

"Even now," she said, "I cannot think about it without an overwhelming feeling of relief. I settled down into the household. The work was hard, I had no regular hours for the Baron would sometimes want to start work very early in the morning or continue until long after midnight.

"On other occasions he would go away and I would have little if anything to do for perhaps three weeks on end.

"It was lucky that I had no friends in Berlin and no inclination to make any, for it was quite impossible to arrange appointments of any sort; I had no private life.

"Sometimes at eight o'clock when I was sitting down in my room to dinner on a tray he would send a message to say he wished me to dine downstairs with a party at eight-thirty.

"I'd have a wild scramble to get into my best frock, to arrange my hair, and to appear in the drawing-room calm and composed by eight-twenty-five.

"Sometimes he allowed me even less time, yet I always succeeded in obeying his orders. It was a kind of game with me not to be outwitted by him. If people were afraid of him he bullied them mercilessly.

"I have seen men go into his room for an interview and come out twenty minutes later white and shaking; he sapped their confidence. Psychologically, I suppose, somehow it was inevitable in the little man.

"He knew that his strength could never be physical, it must be mental. He was inordinately vain and he bought himself a title.

"There were a lot of people who were afraid of him and he knew it. I was, perhaps, the only member of his household who refused to cringe when he was in a bad temper.

"I would never allow myself to be afraid of telling him the truth however unpleasant it might be. He began to respect me, I knew that, yet all the time I was careful not to be too daring or audacious with him.

"He had a quick temper and would fly out at servants, giving them their wages and having them turned out of the house. He never regretted what he had done, in fact, once had committed an action he never wasted another thought on it.

"He had few friends, a great many enemies, and his house was continually crowded with acquaintances of all types and classes. He lived in almost medieval style.

"When I look back on it now it seems almost fantastic, the money that was spent on entertaining, the luxury and extravagance of the whole household.

"It was rather like living in a fairy-tale, Frank, one of those rather sugary German fairy-tales I used to love as a child."

It seemed indeed a fairy-tale to Frank that Helga with her loveliness could have been so efficient as to suit the man she described.

It was ridiculous, of course, to think that women were not as capable of work as men, yet Helga, so feminine and so utterly desirable, seemed meant for all that was beautiful, easy and luxurious in life.

Frank, looking at her now in the rosy light of the lamp behind her head, realized that under her beauty, which in the passing years seemed to have grown more spiritual.

There was, too, a new resilience and strength about her which made it even more compelling.

When he had first seen her earlier in the day he had thought that the years had exacted no toll from her, instead that she appeared younger.

The struggle for independence had deepened Helga's beauty.

"You were living in a fairy-tale," Frank said, "while

I had gone to Canada and was grappling with a very different type of existence."

"My poor dear," Helga said.

"Go on," Frank said. "I want to hear everything right up to today."

Helga hesitated.

"This was all in the beginning of 1913," she said. "Even then we heard rumours of war. In Berlin they talked about it, they drank to it, I think they even dreamed of it. The Baron was opposed to it in every way, he was almost pacifist in his views.

"At any rate he believed that peace was the only recipe for prosperity and that no nation had anything to gain by piracy.

"In his paper he fiercely denounced those people who were preparing Germany by subtle propaganda for the world domination they desired. The Army loathed him, for he laughed at them and derided them.

"He was clever enough not to offend the Kaiser openly, he always agreed, sent flattering messages, and after a few weeks continued as he had done before.

"He was enormously rich, and in the provinces, where his attitude appealed to the ordinary men and women, immensely powerful.

"But even I grew alarmed at the hatred he was arousing among the more powerful politicians, and those in command of the forces. They loathed him with a personal bitterness which showed so obviously when they met him, that at times I wondered that a man of such small stature was not afraid of them being physically aggressive.

"But still he went on. The strange thing was, it was not because of Christian principles or an innate goodness which made him want to turn his country's mind from war, it was a personal dislike of violence.

"He believed in peace as a policy, but it was more than that. He detested anything disruptive or brutal.

"No one who knew him could possibly call him a

coward; he seemed to have courage enough for fifty men and he certainly showed it through the whole of his life.

"But actually I suppose there was in his make-up a fear of being physically man-handled and this, magnified by his extraordinary character, became the driving impulse of his whole life.

"The mere idea of war, of man killing man, tortured his imagination until he felt that he must stop it at any cost.

"It is difficult to understand and still more difficult to put into words, but that was, I believe, the truth that lay behind his attitude and what actually became his mission."

Helga paused and gave a deep sigh.

"And so," she said slowly, "he went on, regardless of all warnings, in spite of what was inevitable."

There was a silence.

"And what did you do?" Frank asked.

"I married him," she said quietly.

* * *

Frank woke, and immediately the realization that something unusual and exciting had happened, with thoughts of Helga, came flooding to his mind.

It was with difficulty that he prevented himself from getting out of bed and going straight to the suite below to convince himself that he had not been dreaming, and that she was really there.

He had gone to bed feeling that he must lie awake all night thinking about her, but he had been tired with a happy exhaustion after the excitement of the day and he had slept peacefully.

The sunshine, pointing shafts of golden light through his half-drawn curtains, had awakened him.

He had left her early the previous night because she had insisted. Before the story she was telling him was finished, and long before Frank had any intention of moving, Helga had risen to her feet.

"It's half-past ten, dear," she said. "You must go."

"But that's ridiculous!" he protested, surprised nonetheless that the time had gone so fast. "Do you mean to say that after all these years of separation you are going to turn me out now? I haven't begun to talk to you yet, or even to realize that I have found you again."

"There's tomorrow," Helga said gently.

"And the next day and the day after that, pray God!" Frank said, "but don't make me go now."

"I must," Helga said firmly. "I have got an important letter to write which must catch the mid-night post."

"To your husband?" Frank asked jealously.

"And also," Helga went on, ignoring his interruption, "I think it's a mistake for you to be in my room so late."

"Good heavens!" Frank said in surprise. "Why does that matter?"

"You don't know the people in this hotel," Helga said. "I do. There's one couple in particular who would be only too delighted to make mischief about me. They've already done everything in their power to be as disagreeable as possible."

"You mean the Loders," Frank said.

"How did you know?" Helga asked.

"I have already spent five days in their company," Frank answered, "and I gathered from them that you weren't exactly popular."

Helga shuddered.

"They were hateful to me," she said. "I understand their feelings—they are English and I am German—but oh, Frank! I hope and pray I shall never treat any human being with such deliberate beastliness whatever their nationality."

"Damn them!" Frank exclaimed.

At the anger in his voice Helga turned and smiled at him.

"Thank you," she said. "That's what I feel, but all the same you mustn't be too obviously friendly with me or they'll make you suffer too."

"It doesn't worry me what they say or think," Frank answered.

"I'm comfortable here," Helga went on. "I've lived in so many different hotels this last year or so, that I find this one peaceful and very beautiful. I don't want to go."

"Why should you?" Frank asked.

"If there was anything that they could use against me, they would complain to the proprietor and threaten to leave unless I went away. They are habitués, they bring a lot of custom—I think in the circumstances I should be the one to suffer."

"It's absurd!" Frank said hotly.

"Nevertheless, my dear, let's avoid such a possibility," Helga said wearily. "We will meet in the morning."

Frank had to do as he was asked. He rose to his feet and moved towards the door, Helga at his side.

As he paused to say good night to her he made a movement as though he would take her in his arms, but she stepped back, away from him.

"No, Frank, no," she said, hardly above a whisper; and in a voice which seemed to him to break on a sob she added: "We mustn't."

For a moment she raised her eyes to his and he saw they were full of tears.

As if she were torn by some emotion which she could not control she turned away from him; without another word she went into her bedroom and closed the door decisively behind her.

Alone in his room Frank pondered, striving to find some explanation. Was she afraid of her husband? Had he been mistaken and was she really in love with him?

He was perplexed, not a little bewildered; yet nothing could depress him, nothing detract from the fact that after all these years he had found Helga.

199

He was close to her again, seeing her, hearing her voice, watching those lips he had loved and kissed so often curve into a smile.

It was only as he was going to sleep that he remembered the letter of which she had spoken, the important letter to catch the midnight post.

She must have gone straight from him, agitated and near to tears, to write it. Why was it important, to whom was it addressed?

Frank guessed that when it was written she would put on a dark coat and walk swiftly from the hotel to the little village post-office.

As he thought of the letter, all the suspicions which had first driven him into seeking acquaintance with the unknown Mrs. Caylor came to his mind to confuse and harry him and to make him desperately afraid.

"It isn't possible," he told himself, "for Helga to be a spy."

At the same time she was a German and, as she had told him that night, had been married to one. Surely this second marriage to an Englishman must have made her, if no less patriotic, at least neutral.

But if she cared for her husband would she have remained apart from him during all these long years of war?

Frank was well aware that the position of German wives in England was not a happy one, but it was not insupportable, especially for someone like Helga who spoke English perfectly and had lived several years of her life there.

Anyway, had she chosen that course her existence could not have been lonelier than it was at present, a woman drifting by herself from hotel to hotel in a strange country. What prospect could be less inviting?

But he could not, dared not, think there was some other reason for Helga's choice.

While he still shrank from admitting that Helga's attitude might be consistent with what he most feared he fell asleep.

As he dressed, a sudden idea made him scribble a short note to Helga. He rang for the valet.

"Take this to Mrs. Caylor in room number twelve," he said.

Anxiously he waited for her answer. In the note he had put:

It's a lovely day. I can't waste a minute of it or you. Let's escape before the gossips are up and about. If you will meet me at the end of the drive in fifteen minutes I know a little place farther up the mountain-side where we can get breakfast.

He had not signed the note, neither did he commence it with her name or any term of endearment. He had a feeling that this was symbolic of their attitude to each other.

There was between them some undercurrent, some strange tempest of emotion which sooner or later would break all the barriers of convention and force them both to face each other truthfully.

Until this happened Frank was content to wait, to let Helga evade him as she was obviously trying to do, strong in his instinct that eventually it would be impossible for them not to belong to each other.

In three minutes the valet returned. Frank almost snatched the note from the tray, his eagerness could not wait. There was one word inscribed on the sheet of paper—"*Ja.*"

"Thank you," Frank said to the valet.

But after the door had closed behind the man he stared at the paper in his hand for a long time. Her acceptance of his invitation was what he wanted, but he felt there was something significant in the fact that she had answered him in her own language.

Was Helga deliberately striving to accentuate the barrier of nationality between them? What other reason could she have for writing in German?

Frank put the note into his breast pocket and chucked the envelope into the waste-paper basket.

Six minutes before the appointed time he walked down the drive to the gates of the hotel. Fir trees screened the entrance from any curious eyes that might have been looking out.

The narrow white road which led one way into the village, continued in the other direction up the mountain, growing steeper and more precarious.

Leaning against the gate-post Frank lit a cigarette and looked over the vista which lay before him.

There was the sweet tinkling of cow-bells and a black-and-white goat accompanied by three kids stopped eating at the other side of the road to stare at him defensively in case he should interfere with her children.

"A land flowing with milk and honey," he thought to himself.

He looked up to see Helga approaching him, her head bare in the sunshine.

"Thank you for coming," he said, and kissed the hand she offered him.

In silence they turned up the road together, moving slowly because of Frank's crutches.

Two days before, Frank taking a stroll with George Loder, had noticed on the hillside several bright orange umbrellas in the garden of a small wooden chalet.

"That looks unusually gay for this primitive scene," he had said.

"It attracts the tourists," Loder said. "They cook quite well and they make an excellent cheese from their own cows. I sometimes walk up there to get it for my wife. I should think they've had a pretty poor season, the war's played havoc with the holiday traffic."

Frank had remembered the chalet when he had sent his invitation to Helga and half an hour later they were sitting under one of the orange umbrellas, sampling home-churned butter and rolls hot from the oven.

They were both hungry; Frank, looking up from his plate, said:

"Thank heaven for a healthy appetite!"

As he watched her smile in response and met the shining radiance of her eyes, he felt a flood of almost unbearable happiness course through him.

"Oh, my sweet," he whispered, unable to stop himself, "I'm so happy."

As if he had dealt her an unexpected blow, he watched the smile fade from her lips and her eyes cloud before she turned away from him.

There was a sense of restraint between them, but later, when they had finished breakfast and moved farther up the mountain-side to a secluded spot under the trees Helga seemed to forget what was troubling her.

They sat down on the grass among the blue, yellow, and crimson flowers. Watching a small curly-tailed squirrel go scrambling away from them in fear along the branches of a great fir tree. Frank had the idea that Helga too would run from him if she could.

He was very gentle with her, asking no questions, trying to keep the conversation commonplace.

It was not difficult for there crept over them both a physical joy in being in each other's company which, whatever their mental disturbances, drew them together so that they laughed gaily like children.

"We might be all alone on a curve of the world," Helga said suddenly.

"We are," Frank answered. "Why remember anything else but this? Everything that is past is forgotten and there may never be a future. Let's think of us, you and I, here and now."

Helga lay back on the grass, her hands behind her head, her eyes looking up into the cloudless blue sky above them.

"Is it possible ever to forget everything?" she asked, and Frank, leaning on his elbow beside her, bent towards her lips.

"Everything but this," he answered, and kissed her.

Just for a moment he thought she would resist him, then her arms were round his neck drawing him closer, letting the passion of his kisses wake a like response in her.

It was a moment of ecstasy, of rapture which was almost agony in its intensity. Only as they touched each other did they realize how the wounds of their severance had never healed in those long years.

"Oh, my darling, my darling, my own," Frank murmured.

He kissed her eyes, the soft hollow of her neck, and he felt her quiver and tremble beneath his touch.

Suddenly he put his head down against her breast and fought against the tears which threatened to overwhelm him.

It was too much, overpowering, this reunion with the only woman he had ever loved, the only beautiful and perfect thing he had known in his life.

He felt her hands stroking his head and knew from the tumult of her breast that she could not speak, that she was overcome as he was.

How long they sat there they did not know.

They wanted only to touch each other; to savour the indescribable comfort in that they were together. The world beyond themselves was forgotten.

Finally Helga reminded Frank that they had not eaten for a long time.

She knelt beside him on the grass, striving to restore order to the curls he had untidied. He watched her as she looked into the tiny mirror she carried in her bag.

Her cheeks were flushed, her eyes shining, her lips parted in that secret half-smile of happiness that women wear when they have been kissed by someone they love.

"I adore you," he said to her.

"I love you . . ." she whispered.

There has never been anyone but you," he told her.

"You are all I have ever longed for and dreamt about in one person and now I have found you again."

She saw the question in his eyes, but he knew that for the moment she would not answer it.

They had a ridiculous meal of eggs, cheese, and coffee at the little chalet. As they faced each other under the orange umbrella, they were too happy to talk.

Frank watched Helga as if he were afraid to take his eyes for one moment from her loveliness, and she flushed, sighed, and then smiled at the love he could not hide from her.

The strength of it and the electrical magnetism of his adoration made her unable to prevent her hand from creeping into his, her eyes from being drawn to his with a longing in them that would not be denied.

Only as the sun sank lower in the heavens and they turned their faces reluctantly homewards did the glory of her happiness seem dimmed.

As they drew nearer to the hotel Helga shivered. They went upstairs to her sitting-room.

When the door was closed behind them Frank would have taken her again into his arms, but she made the excuse that she must tidy herself, and left him alone.

She was away what seemed to him a long time.

He wandered restlessly round the room. Waiting for her on the table were two letters which must have arrived by the afternoon post.

Almost without thinking he glanced at the one on top and noted that the postmark over a French stamp was Rouen.

Frank wandered towards the window and looked out and as he stood there a girl whom he had not seen before came out on to the terrace. She arranged one of the chairs in a comfortable position so that it got the full rays of the setting sun.

She had very fair hair which reminded him of Helga's, but which she wore drawn back behind her ears into a severe and unbecoming roll. He caught a glimpse of her face, not unattractive, and he wondered idly who she was.

A sound at the door made him turn round apprehensively. Helga came in.

She had changed her dress for one of black chiffon, and although it was relieved by a bunch of white flowers at her throat it gave her a somewhat sombre appearance.

Frank felt that the sobriety of the garment destroyed the radiance of the girl who had been with him all day.

She picked up her letters automatically, hardly glancing at them, and Frank knew, even before she spoke, that for some reason she was depressed.

"Who is writing to you from Rouen?" he asked.

She gave an obvious start, looked at the letters in her hand, and said quickly:

"Why have you been looking at my letters?"

"I noticed it quite by chance," Frank answered, "as it lay on the table. Why should you mind?"

Helga looked at him.

"It doesn't matter," she said. "I'm sorry."

"Come here," Frank said.

She came slowly towards him. When she stood beside him he put his hand on her shoulder and looked into her face.

"What are you hiding from me, Helga?" he asked tenderly. "Why are you afraid?"

"I'm not," she protested. "I am not."

He knew she lied, knew also that she was trembling, but he would not let her go.

"Tell me," he said; as she did not answer he added, "Is it this husband of yours?"

A strange expression flickered across Helga's face and suddenly something told Frank what he wanted to know. He tightened his grip on her shoulder until it must have hurt her.

"Answer me, Helga," he said, "I want the truth. You have no husband."

For a moment he thought she would defy him, would deny wildly and in anger what he had suggested, then she covered her face with her hands and her whole body sagged as if beneath a blow.

He knew the answer to his question; as the realization of what she had admitted flashed to his mind he heard his voice saying with a calmness which surprised him:

"And so, under the guise of being married to an Englishman, Helga, you are spying for Germany."

He heard Helga give a gasp. There was a silence which had in it horror and a terror which gripped Frank so that he stood immobile as if turned to stone.

Then with an agonized shuddering cry as of a child, Helga flung her arms around him and buried her face against him.

His arms went round her even while he had no feeling, no emotion left, only a numb misery which encompassed his whole being.

With great sobs shaking her whole body, in a voice broken and tortured, Helga was saying:

"Help me . . . Frank, oh, for pity's sake . . . help me!"

CHAPTER TWELVE

Helga, with her face half hidden in Frank's shoulder, spoke in a voice so low that at times he could hardly hear what she said, yet he feared to interrupt her. His arms held her tightly to him.

"You must tell me everything," he had commanded.

She obeyed, crouched on the sofa beside him, her fingers occasionally clutching desperately at the lapels of his tweed coat as if only by clinging to him could she gain the strength to continue.

"After I had married the Baron . . ." she began then said, "You will think it strange for me not to call him by his Christian name. Somehow I always thought of him as the Baron, he was never . . . my husband except in name.

"I looked after him as I had done previously, managing the household and still doing a great part of his secretarial work.

"He was fond of me in his own way; when he remembered my existence as an individual apart from him he was exceedingly kind, but he was never what one might call considerate. I was happy in my new security, and perfectly content in the interest which I had in him and his work.

"When he asked me to marry him I thought that per-

sonal intimacy would play a very small part . . . or none
. . . in our marriage, and I was right.

"He liked having me there, he clung to my youth, he
was proud of my looks; what was more, I know that I
was able to give him a companionship which he had
never found before in either man or woman.

"Then came this war. Germany was in a turmoil, all
that was familiar and secure seeming to vanish overnight. It was a crushing blow for the Baron although he
had anticipated it for years.

"For the first time I realized his age and that his vitality lay not in years, but in the strength of his personality.

"For a few days he did not move from his study and
it was then that he conceived and wrote the vehement
revolutionary articles which were to bring about his
downfall.

"He did not consult me about them. Perhaps he realized that I should have begged him to be cautious, fore-
seeing to some extent the wrath which would inflame
his enemies, who were waiting for just such an opportunity.

"Germany was in a fever of excitement, martial law
was in force, the very people who most disliked my husband were supremely powerful.

"He was arrested and taken away. I shall never forget that morning—it was a nightmare of which I can't
speak even now without feeling again the horror and
humiliation of it.

"They hadn't even the decency to treat my husband
as befitted his rank and position, they behaved as
though he were a common criminal—a murderer could
not have been handled more roughly or treated worse.

"They wouldn't allow him to take with him any of his
personal belongings.

"When he was gone the house was invaded by soldiers, who, having searched everywhere for documents

209

that might be used as evidence against my husband, locked the doors of the main rooms and dismissed the staff.

"I and one old maid were told that for the present we were to remain in occupation of two rooms at the top of the house. There we were kept for several months, virtually prisoners.

"I wrote letters, I pleaded with those officers who constituted themselves my warders to be allowed to see my husband, or failing that to be given work of some sort, nursing or even factory work, to take my mind off the tragedy of my own life.

"No notice was taken of me in any way. I was not allowed to leave the house except for an hour's daily walk in the private gardens at the back.

"I had no news of any sort from outside. It was an experience I hope never to live through again and I was afraid . . . Frank, horribly, terribly . . . afraid."

She stopped speaking for a moment. Frank felt her trembling as she hid her face against him.

"Hush, darling," he said, soothing her and drawing her still closer to him.

With an effort Helga continued.

"At last I was informed that my husband was dead. Later I learnt how he had died—of privation and from bad treatment. I was still kept in close confinement until one day quite unexpectedly I was sent for to the library downstairs.

"I had not been into the room since my husband's arrest. Many valuable things had been taken away, pictures had been torn from the walls.

"There was a fine marquetry cabinet which had contained a collection of snuff-boxes. It had had its glass doors smashed.

"Sitting in my husband's chair, the one he had always used, was a man whom I recognized. He had been for several years an important member of the Government and one of the Army chiefs.

"He fixed an eyeglass in his eye as I entered and looked me up and down as though I were cattle brought for his inspection.

" 'So this is the Baroness,' he said.

"With a snap of his fingers he dismissed the soldiers who had brought me to the room.

"There was a thin, bespectacled man sitting at my husband's desk who occasionally took notes of what was said, otherwise we were alone. I was not offered a chair, but stood waiting what I fully expected would be a death sentence.

" 'Baroness Hostzal,' the officer started, 'the authorities have for some time been wondering what to do with you.'

"He paused as if expecting me to speak, but I remained silent, staring at him across the room, showing, I hope, none of the fear which made my legs tremble and my mouth dry.

" 'Your husband,' the officer continued, 'enemy of the Emperor, of his Government, and of the German nation, is dead. He was not shot as he should have been for being a traitor to the Fatherland, but he died naturally.

" 'It has been decided, therefore, that the mercy which was extended to him shall also be extended to you.

" 'We intend to give you a chance to serve your country and in some part, if you can, to mitigate the harm done by your husband. You are very fortunate, Baroness.'

"I made no reply, and impatiently he asked:

" 'You are agreeable?'

" 'I cannot answer that question until I know what you require of me,' I answered.

"The officer lit a cigarette, regarding me all the time.

" 'We have been making enquiries about you,' he went on, 'and find that for some years you were resident in England. Do you speak English well?'

211

" 'Yes,' I answered.

" 'You have friends there?'

" 'None.'

"My answer seemed to surprise him.

" 'In the last years,' he questioned, 'you have not communicated with anyone?'

" 'No one,' I said firmly.

"He frowned, then his brow cleared.

" 'Nevertheless,' he said, 'you speak English fluently. That is important. You know English life and English customs.'

"He seemed to expect some sort of answer to this, and I inclined my head.

" 'Very well, then, Baroness, these are your orders. You will be given an English passport with which you will proceed at once to Switzerland. You will live there as the German wife of an Englishman who is serving his country in France.

" 'You will let it be known that you have separated only because of your nationality and because you personally wish to take no part in the war, either for or against your own country.

" 'From time to time you will receive letters from various parts of France, from England, or from Belgium. These you will forward to an address which will be given to you.

" 'Their contents will obviously be discussed with no one and you will always post the envelope in which you forward them personally.'

"For a moment I could not quite understand what he meant, then I gasped:

" 'I am to be a spy!'

"The officer smiled.

" 'It is the perquisite of many pretty women, Baroness.'

" 'But I can't,' I said, 'I can't do such a thing. I could never carry it out. My lies would be discovered, apart from the fact that I . . .'

"I stopped. I was going to say 'Apart from the fact that I don't want to work for a country which has murdered my husband,' but I didn't have the courage to say it when it came to the point.

"These two men staring at me with cruel merciless eyes—I knew that if I defied them I should be swept from their path as if I were some insignificant animal, got rid of as easily as my husband had been.

"The officer put out his cigarette and rose to his feet.

" 'So,' he said, 'you prefer to remain here. Is life in an attic so very attractive? But your privacy will soon be invaded, I'm afraid. This charming mansion will be required in the near future.'

" 'Prison!' I thought. 'That means prison!' I remembered all the terrible tales I had been told of what German prisons were like, of the treatment of the inmates, of the cruelty of those in command. I couldn't face it, Frank, I couldn't.

" 'No, no,' I said, and I know my hands were trembling. 'Give me time to think, to consider.'

" 'We are at war, Baroness,' the officer reminded me sternly, 'and decisions, small or big, have to be made at once.'

"He saw that I had made up my mind. I had no choice. He drew from his pocket a passport which already bore my name, photograph, description, and was identical with those issued by the British Government. I was described as Helga Marlowe, wife of Captain Basil Marlowe.

"That night I left for Lucerne, and it was only when I had crossed the frontier and came to the peace and quiet of this country that I broke down and cried bitterly. I knew then that I hated my country, loathed the people in it, yet I was bound to them by bonds from which I could never escape.

"When the first letter came to me written from France I kept it for nearly thirty-six hours. Should I throw it in the fire, I thought, destroy it and then myself? I read it. It was in code—they all are—ostensibly an order for silk from a firm at Lyons.

"Finally I posted it as I had been told. Three days later I received a communication which said: 'Dear Madam. Your order has been received and shall be attended to without delay.'

"The last two words had been underlined and I knew they contained a message for me and a threat. I was watched, then. I was not free as I had for a moment imagined.

"Someone knew that that letter had been kept thirty-six hours after the time of its arrival. I was afraid, Frank. I am still afraid."

Helga glanced over her shoulder as she spoke and Frank knew by her white face and her haunted eyes that her fear was very real.

"You are safe enough now," he told her. "I promise you that, my darling."

She looked up at him as if she was longing to believe him, but he saw the doubt in her eyes.

"Any little slip I make," she whispered, "is reported. They know everything I do. Sooner or later I get a warning. Once in Berne I found that the waiter who served me was in their pay.

"Another time a man called to see me pretending to be a relation. They have eyes everywhere—they hear and know everything."

There was a long silence, then in a voice deep with despair Helga continued:

"Twice I have received different passports and been given other names. Marlowe was the first, then I was a Mrs. Barrett, and now Caylor. I have no intimation as to why I am moved, I simply receive instructions and the next day I move on as I am directed."

Helga's head sank lower and in a voice filled with emotion, she said:

"At night I lie awake thinking of the men that I am sending to their death. Oh, my darling, don't you think

214

at times I have imagined that you were among them? These last years have been a terror from which I know there is no escape.

"I can't get away from this country, I can't go back to my own. If I attempted to defy them I should pay the penalty. There was a man who was working for them— I met him and I knew that he was cracking, the strain was too much for him.

"Later I heard that he had been found one morning dead from an overdose of sleeping draught.

"They meant me to know about it, I was supplied with every detail. He was young and he was afraid; he did not want to die, he wanted to live."

Helga's body was swept by a storm of sobbing.

"My darling, my poor one," Frank said. "Don't, please don't. We have got to think, you and I, you mustn't give way now—you've got to be calm and very clever."

He knew that Helga did not exaggerate and that they were up against a force whose strength it would be ridiculous to belittle. Slowly he took his arms from around her and got to his feet.

He walked over to the table and picked up the two letters which had arrived for her by that afternoon's post. She watched him with wide eyes, the tears still wet on her cheeks, as he opened the envelopes.

They were both in code—one apparently a long, friendly letter from a woman in the country to an old friend, the other spoke of the delivery of several pounds of cheese. Frank, having looked at them, put them down again.

"They've got to go tonight," Helga said dully.

She spoke calmly now, calm with the sort of abject misery which sees no hope, no light anywhere through the darkness of despair. Frank put out his hands and drew her to her feet.

"Listen, Helga," he said. "Do you love me?"

There was no need for her to answer, there was a

radiance in her expression and a light in her eyes which transformed her whole face.

Only her lips quivered as she raised them to his. He kissed her gently.

"Then every risk is worth while," he said quietly. "Now attend to me. Tonight we will leave here on the local train for Berne. You will go downstairs now and inform the proprietor that the letters you received this afternoon contained bad news, your husband is wounded, you have to go to him."

"But, Frank—" Helga interrupted.

"There's no but," Frank said. "You've got to do it, Helga. I believe everything you've told me, and I know that I must get you away from here, from this country. From Berne we will go to Genoa and at Genoa we will find a boat which will take us to some neutral country, South America, Java, China, what does it matter?"

He paused before he said positively:

"We will be together and because we love each other we will get through. Do you love me enough?"

Helga opened her arms to him and as if her emotion was too much, too overpowering, she dropped her head and he felt her lips and her tears on his hand.

For a moment he could not speak, but could only hold her close, until turning to him she put her arms about his neck and he felt her heart beating wildly against his.

"And you?" she said at length. "How will you manage?"

"I shall go down to dinner as usual," he replied. "When I have eaten I shall take a stroll down the village. I shall be waiting for you where the houses end. You will seem surprised to see me, will stop the car and ask me to see you off.

"At the station I shall tell the driver that I intend to walk back. It is unlikely that my disappearance will be noticed until breakfast time tomorrow, by which hour we shall have crossed the frontier."

"It can't be true," Helga whispered. "Is this really happening?"

"It is," Frank answered. "I shall not see you again," he continued. "It's wiser not. Be looking out for me, my sweet."

He turned towards the door, then her arms were around him again, drawing his head down to hers, seeking his lips, firing him with the passion that had set her aflame.

For a moment they forgot everything, danger, flight, the unknown future, and remembered nothing save themselves.

"I love you," Helga murmured, her lips against his.

He could feel her whole body trembling but this time not with fear.

"I adore you," Frank cried. "God knows I've missed you—there has never been anyone else but you my precious."

"Oh, Frank . . . Frank!"

Now he was kissing her again, kissing her until the room whirled round them, the world vanished and they were alone in a Paradise of their own.

There was no danger, no treachery, no cruelty, nor hate; only love, that was boundless and elevated, beyond nation, caste or creed.

"I love you my darling . . . I am yours forever," Helga cried.

* * *

"We must be sensible," Frank said a long time later, but his voice shook.

They drew apart.

"Give me one of your suit-cases," he commanded. "I will put my clothes into it and you can label it with yours."

She came to the door with him; as he moved along the corridor towards the next flight of stairs she squared

217

her shoulders, raised her head, and went down below to tell the proprietor the bad news she had received.

Frank, walking along the landing towards his room, saw a woman come out of the door next to his. She stood aside to let him pass, for he was encumbered both by his crutches and the suit-case he carried.

He thanked her and got a demure smile in return.

She was a stranger, yet her face seemed familiar, and he remembered that she was the Scandinavian he had seen standing on the terrace earlier in the evening.

As he got into his room the boom of the gong throughout the hotel proclaimed that seven-thirty dinner was served.

Frank opened the suit-case and was deciding which among his things were the most necessary to him, when he paused and stood still in the centre of the room.

The girl next door had exactly the same colouring as Helga, fair hair and blue eyes, they were also about the same height.

Swiftly he moved towards his door, turned the handle and cautiously looked outside. The corridor was empty. He hesitated, then moving as quickly as he could he opened the door next to his.

It was a small room, and an open box and scattered clothes proclaimed that its occupant had been unpacking.

Frank stood looking about him. Lying on the chest of drawers he saw a large, grey leather handbag. When he opened it he found what he sought—a passport. As he saw the photograph inside he gave a sigh of relief.

He put the passport in his pocket, hurried out of the room and back into his own. The whole transaction had taken less than three minutes and he had not been seen.

He locked his door and examined what he had stolen. The fair-haired girl was a Swede, and she was described as a nurse.

It was an old passport and the photograph had been

taken two or three years before; it was not a good likeness.

Were Helga to draw her hair back from her ears and wear her hat at an unbecoming angle no great difference would be discernible.

Frank put the passport in his pocket. The Swedish consul at Berne would doubtless have a job of work to do in a few days, but that was not his business.

When the suit-case was ready he left it outside Helga's bedroom and went on down to dinner. Almost the last to enter the dining-room, he was greeted by cries of welcome from the Loders.

"Well, you are a stranger!" said George Loder, rising to his feet and clapping him on the back. "We wondered what on earth had happened to you."

"Been taking things a bit quietly," Frank replied. "I got a twinge of the old pain."

"You're like me," Mrs. Loder said. "When I'm ill I want to be alone—except for George, of course."

"Come and have coffee with us after dinner," Loder invited, and Frank, moving towards his own table, promised that he would.

It seemed to him as if the evening were interminable. It was with the greatest difficulty that he prevented himself from looking at his watch every few minutes.

The night was warm and they had coffee on the terrace, Frank conscious all the time that behind him in the hotel were the lighted windows of Helga's rooms.

It was ten o'clock when finally he said good night to the Loders and went upstairs.

He locked his door and taking from his breast pocket the two letters Helga had received that afternoon he placed them in an envelope and addressed it to the number in Savile Row he had been given by Colonel Harrison.

He then made out a telegram which he intended to send from Berne. Decoded, it read,

"Danger effectively disposed of. Writing."

He could not help wondering what Colonel Harrison would think of his methods, at the same time he knew full well that no other course was open to him Helga's safety was all that mattered now.

To Lady Stanbury he wrote fully. He told her how, many years ago, he had loved Helga and how he had found her again. He said that they were going abroad in search of some place of quiet and safety until the war ended.

"Pray God it will not be much longer, now!" he added.

He did not ask her to show the letter to her cousin, but he knew that she would do so.

When the letters were ready Frank went downstairs. In the hall he saw the proprietor closing up the reception-desk for the night.

He held the letters prominently so that the man could see them and would know where he was going.

"Good night," he said in passing.

"Good night, *mein Herr*," the proprietor replied.

There was no need to hurry, and the night was warm. The deep purple shadows thrown by a small moon crept up the star-strewn sky.

In their lighted rooms the village familes ate their evening meal—Frank could see their smiling faces through the uncurtained windows as he passed and occasionally hear a burst of laughter.

He walked on until he came to the last house. There was a little bridge and he leant against it, listening to the tinkle of the water as it cascaded over the stones, on its swift way to the distant meadowlands.

It was very quiet. He was aware that his heart was beating, his whole being alert and yearning for the coming of Helga.

Life was beginning for him at last. He was thirty-eight, he had roved, striven and struggled in the past, now finally he had found what perhaps he had sought for all these years.

The future, as yet unwritten, might hold for them danger, privations, and further struggles, but they would be together.

"Helga."

Frank started when he realized that he had spoken her name aloud.

There was only the deep silence of the moonlight night to answer him, the fragrance of field flowers and the whisper of a rising breeze in the pine trees.

"I love you," he whispered. "Come quickly. Oh, my precious darling, come quickly.

"Helga!" he called again, but this time soundlessly, with the yearning of his whole being.

Then he saw the lights of an approaching car and knew that he was answered.

Helga was coming to him. He was beginning again, but this time a life with love.